Dancing in Damascus

SUNY series,
The Margins of Literature

Mihai I. Spariosu, editor

Dancing in Damascus

☙ Stories ☙

Nancy Lindisfarne

State University of New York Press

Published by
State University of New York Press, Albany

For more information, address the State University of New York Press,
State University Plaza, Albany, NY 12246

Production by Diane Ganeles
Marketing by Anne M. Valentine

Library of Congress Cataloging-in-Publication Data

Lindisfarne, Nancy, 1944–
    Dancing in Damascus : stories / Nancy Lindisfarne.
        p. cm. — (SUNY series, the margins of literature)
    Includes bibliographical references.
    ISBN 0-7914-4635-2 (alk. paper — ISBN 0-7914-4636-0 (pbk. :
alk. paper)
    1. Damascus (Syria)—Social life and customs—Fiction.
    I. Title. II. Series.

PS3562.I51127 D36 2000
813´.54—dc21   99-049702

10 9 8 7 6 5 4 3 2 1

For Edward, Anna, and Ruard
With all love

CONTENTS

Sketch Map of Syria and the Eastern Mediterranean

THE TORTOISE

Omm Kasim was the mother of three sons. Kasim, her eldest, who should have married first, then Bashar, then Faiz. But they were now all back-to-front. What little was left of Omm Kasim's pride in her sons, and her few remaining hopes for herself, vanished when Faiz married the slut. Faiz's wife was a nightmare creature, everything wrong and in reverse. She was anything but a willing bride who'd help around the house and raise children whom Omm Kasim could cherish and who would love her in return.

Omm Kasim now knew that every evening for the rest of her life she would sit in front of the television, while Kasim, Bashar, and Faiz and the slut slumped on

the two long divans, smoking, arguing, switching chan-
nels and demanding that she get them tea and snacks.
Abu Kasim would be there too, but at least he got his own
supper tray from the kitchen.

Every evening too, at about nine o'clock, poor
hunched Zahra would knock timidly at the front door,
then creep unnoticed to her place at the end of the divan
farthest from the television. Omm Kasim used to take
great comfort in being the mother of sons. And she used to
pity Zahra, knowing that if Zahra never came again, the
others would not even think to ask why. But since the ar-
rival of the slut, Omm Kasim wasn't so sure whose life
was worse. The terrible thing about sons, she thought, is
that they are with you for the rest of your life.

Omm Kasim cast back to see if there were any
chances she'd missed, but she found none. Her sister in
Lebanon was preoccupied with her own family, and her
brothers hadn't spoken to her in all the thirty years she'd
been married to Abu Kasim. There were a few cousins who
kept in touch, but only to guarantee themselves a bed
when they came to Damascus. Omm Kasim knew they
didn't see their visits as part of a reciprocal agreement.

Then she thought forward: the odds were that Kasim
and Bashar would take sluttish wives, just as Faiz had
done. After all, what other kind of woman would want to
marry them? And, since none of them would ever find the
money to buy a house of their own, Abu Kasim, ever
proud to be the honest shopkeeper and reliable father,
would support them all—and their children. And he'd
continue to talk about Arab customs and families which
stayed together. She sighed. Abu Kasim had been dashing
when she'd eloped with him and stuffed a pillow under
her skirt so the judge would marry them, but Abu Kasim's
courage had crept away, leaving him ineffectual and con-
sumed with worry for their sons.

Each lunchtime, when Kasim returned from the night
shift driving the taxi, Abu Kasim would quip, "Work well,
eat well, eh?" Each lunchtime, Kasim would reply with a
silent snarl.

Or, sometimes, Abu Kasim would try praise: "It's good Kasim has a real job. Now you boys—Bashar, Faiz—need to follow his example. We all must watch out. You know what they say: that when the government puts its hands on things, people get lazy."

He meant well, Omm Kasim knew that, but he never noticed the murderous scowls on the faces of their two younger sons. Omm Kasim sank round-shouldered into her chair. "Others would be broken, would be slaves by now. But we Syrians are resilient." Abu Kasim said this too often these days and each time Omm Kasim wanted to cry. It was as close as her husband would get to admitting that their three precious sons had become sad, helpless men.

Omm Kasim turned back to the television, knowing no one had noticed her attention straying in the first place.

The next day Omm Kasim found the usual morning-after debris waiting for her when she switched on the single dangling bulb in the tiny kitchen. Pots and pans, plates, glasses, melon rinds, grease and tea leaves all swam in the dark gray concrete sink. She made coffee for each of them as they appeared, sleep-swollen, sour and foul-mouthed. When she finally managed to clear the small wooden counter and the second ring of the stove, she began preparing lunch. She hardly cared that she was still in her nightdress.

She retrieved the leftovers from the stink of the ancient fridge, then chopped vegetables and put the potatoes on to boil. Each lunchtime she tried to serve them something different: fried eggplant, courgettes in yogurt, and sometimes even special dishes like *mallubeh bi tajaj*, though Kasim of course ate only hamburgers and chips.

Kasim returned at noon. "Where have you put my papers?" he shouted as he stomped down the long hallway to the table in the open court at the center of the house. Omm Kasim scurried to collect the papers from the chair where he'd strewn them the day before. They were for some course in Cyprus. What he really wanted, Omm

Kasim knew, was to do black market work and a part-time degree.

The cutlery, cold leftovers, and a fresh salad were already on the table. Kasim pushed them aside and spread out the application forms, clearly resenting the scraps of his life they asked him to reveal. Then, after a few moments, he bellowed, "Where's my food?" He didn't bother to look up until she handed him the hamburger wrapped in two flat rounds of bread. "Watch out. Don't you dare spill anything here."

"I'm doing my best; I do it for you."

Omm Kasim looked at her son's bearlike shoulders, flabby, covered with wiry black hairs, and his puffy, unshaven face. She wondered if other mothers were also repelled by their children.

By this time, Bashar and Faiz and the slut had also come to the table. Bashar picked at his food, then moaned about a headache and demanded a tray in his room. He'd never been completely right since his road accident five years ago. But there wasn't that much wrong with him either, beyond soul-deep sloth.

Faiz and the slut had already started on the stew when Abu Kasim returned from the shop. He was carrying a watermelon, pleased with his contribution to the meal. To annoy his father, Faiz reached over to fondle the slut and they joked about the onions in the stew and how they'd fart all through the siesta. Then, unfortunately for Omm Kasim, Faiz glanced up and saw her hovering near the kitchen door. "We've told you not to use so many onions. Don't you ever learn?"

"I put in only one onion this time," Omm Kasim replied. "We said no onions," hissed the slut, and Abu Kasim, for lack of will, nodded his pained agreement.

Omm Kasim clutched the knife that she was using to carve the watermelon and her voice rose and then broke, "Tomorrow our new bride will cook lunch." But Faiz and the slut only snorted. Omm Kasim knew they knew that she would always be there to cook for them.

The only unexpected part of lunch was the knock at the door before they'd finished the melon. Anwar, who always beamed his hellos, looked in from the street, grinning. "Ah, I knew my mother-in-law loved me," he said, using the conventional joke to invite himself to the meal.

Omm Kasim guessed that Anwar only dropped in because of her cooking but, given Kasim's pride in his popularity, neither Anwar, nor anyone else, would ever say as much. Kasim and Anwar had been at high school together.

Anwar repaired TVs. He was from Houran and Omm Kasim couldn't resist asking him, "Which is worse, no sugar or no tea?" It was a rationing joke that no sweet-toothed Hourani could have missed, but Anwar answered good-heartedly, "No sugar, of course," and Omm Kasim suddenly felt like a more valuable person. When Anwar was there the others had to keep their sniggers to themselves and they soon got bored. Omm Kasim watched as one after the other they went for their afternoon naps. Or, in the case of Faiz and the slut, their afternoon fuck. She was pleased for the chance to share a pot of mint tea with Anwar.

Omm Kasim tried not to disturb Abu Kasim when she finally lay down on her side of the double bed, but he woke anyway and she watched her husband through half-closed eyes as he trundled across the bedroom. He looked old as he smoothed his silver hair round the bald patch. His pudgy belly looked absurd swaddled in a white cotton vest tucked tightly into his underpants. A ripping fart roared out from the toilet next to the kitchen. Serves him right, she thought, for condoning the vicious jokes about the stew.

He shits and is afraid of being hungry, Omm Kasim remembered the old saying and the dart of malice changed something and made her feel more comfortable with her own soft, white body.

That evening everything seemed the same. But when Zahra slipped in, Omm Kasim had a hard look at the old woman. No, not that old, she corrected herself, only a little older than me and she wondered if, like Zahra, she too was so faded she was almost invisible.

Zahra's dull green dress made her bosom look like a stuffed marrow, as if she'd nursed an army of kids. But Zahra had no one—no children, no husband, nothing. Omm Kasim remembered her own horror when Zahra had explained how, just after her husband died, some of his relatives had moved in to help her out and then, after only a few weeks, they offered to help her further by buying her share of the house. Poor Zahra, Omm Kasim thought, she never even got as far as anger when later they'd heard how the relatives had built a small hotel on the land near Merjay Square where Zahra's house had been. That was why Zahra had moved from the center of Damascus to Shamsiyyah, though Omm Kasim found she could no longer remember what tenuous connection now made them Zahra's closest kin.

During a commercial, Kasim flicked the television over to the Egyptian soap opera and Omm Kasim noticed Zahra straighten up to watch. She too clearly enjoyed the drama of Dr. Rauf and Poppy's marriage and when Kasim flipped back to the American film with its tiresome subtitles, Zahra sagged back on the cushions.

"Turn it back to Dr. Rauf," Omm Kasim said, "that's what we want to watch." It was the first time anyone had included Zahra in one of the nightly quarrels. Of course, Kasim refused and as Omm Kasim shrugged, she felt aggrieved for Zahra as well as herself.

Early the next evening, after the siesta, when Abu Kasim had returned to his shop and the rest of them had left for their stroll, Omm Kasim put on her heavy stockings, her street coat, and scarf and made a visit to Zahra's tiny house, which was tucked into the hillside just around the corner.

Omm Kasim lifted the brass door knocker, a small, elegant Ottoman lady's hand, and let it fall back gently. Zahra greeted Omm Kasim fearfully, anticipating bad news. When Omm Kasim said simply, "I'm always so busy. I should have visited earlier," a bemused Zahra ushered her through a narrow hall to a tiny front room. In her turn she mumbled the expected greetings almost as if she'd forgotten what they should be. She pointed Omm Kasim toward the divan which stood along the wall and sat down herself on one of the wooden chairs which flanked the table in front of the window. They were silent until Omm Kasim said, "I like flowers too," nodding toward the sad begonias which shared Zahra's view of the street.

Zahra started, remembering what should happen next. "Would you like coffee?" she asked, leaving Omm Kasim to contemplate the dull prints of Mecca and the tourist board calendar on the yellowed wall. On a shelf in the corner there was a Bakelite radio. Zahra had switched it off before she'd opened the door.

Zahra returned with a small round tray. Omm Kasim's coffee was so sweet that she wondered what might be left of Zahra's sugar ration. Zahra took an ornate, old-fashioned box from the shelf and offered Omm Kasim *malabas*, sugared almonds which were gray and cracked; they might have been leftovers from Zahra's own wedding.

Omm Kasim and Zahra struggled round the conventions of a visit. How could Omm Kasim ask, 'How is your family?' when Zahra's only answer would be, 'What family? You're all I've got.' And if Zahra asked her the same question, what could she reply except, 'Do you mean Faiz and the slut?'

But Zahra surprised Omm Kasim: "I have a little garden," she said. She led Omm Kasim down the hallway past a dark cupboard of a kitchen and an even smaller bathroom, then up narrow stairs. The glazed door at the top opened onto a small square of earth bounded on either side by the much larger neighboring houses and by the pale yellow stone of the hillside at the back. In the garden there was a chair and some trays of *malukhiyya*, whose leaves had dried dark green in the sun. There were also a few hollyhocks and a small rounded fig tree growing out of the stone.

"There is a lot to do for winter," Omm Kasim commented, nodding at the *malukhiyya*.

Having visited Zahra made it easier for Omm Kasim to leave the house the next morning. After making their coffee, Omm Kasim allowed the debris to swim in the sink and changed into her street dress. She'd decided to shop in Sikke for the first time in years. At least, she told herself, the green beans would be a few lira cheaper than the *fasuuuuuuuliyaah* of the raucous street seller.

At first she was overwhelmed by the energy of the women who bustled along the high street. Then she remembered that she too could elbow her way to the front of the shops and insist on the good tomatoes which were kept hidden under the counter. As Omm Kasim trudged back up the hill, the weight of her shopping was lightened by the thought that she must have saved five, perhaps even ten, lira by venturing out. By the time she had slipped back into the house and put the coins in the little purse she kept under her side of the mattress, she was very pleased with herself indeed.

In the weeks that followed, Omm Kasim often walked down to the high street past the giant eucalyptus and the canaries which chorused from the balcony of the house on the corner opposite. But what she really enjoyed was stashing ten lira under the mattress after each expedition. No one at home noticed her new routine, or if they did, they didn't care.

Once after she'd returned from shopping, she tried to slip out again to see Zahra. But Kasim had rushed to the door and shouted, "Come back! It's nearly lunchtime." Omm Kasim had no choice but to submit to his bellow and of course the neighbors had watched as she returned to the house, crumpled and humiliated. After that, she learned to stop at Zahra's before she set off shopping and Zahra, who'd never quite managed to get down to the high street shops before, began to come with her.

Some time later Omm Kasim tried another strategy. She put on her street dress and coat after the siesta. She was prepared when Kasim challenged her. She shrilled in a voice that would sear eardrums and cleave the gossips' tongues in two, "Zahra is ill and I'm going to visit her." Thereafter, had Kasim been more observant, he might have wondered about Zahra's strange illness, which so often struck her down in the early evening, but allowed her up in time for television at Abu Kasim's.

Over the next weeks Omm Kasim made cuttings from the lemon geraniums which grew on the balcony, and took them to Zahra's. She also bought some bruised plums and took some sugar with her when she visited. Together they had made a few jars of plum jam which stayed with Zahra and added a rich spot of color to her kitchen. Zahra too contributed what she could and one day, heaven knows how, she produced several kilos of new pistachios which they husked in the little garden, their hands reddening with the work. "These are good for the brain," Zahra said. "Good for thinking," and they both understood what she meant.

Then, later, Omm Kasim stole one of the slut's old magazines which lay gathering dust under the divan. Some women Omm Kasim had overheard talking at the butcher's had said the best bit was the doctor's advice page.

"Just listen to this," Omm Kasim said, selecting one of the letters.

Zahra listened with horror and then suddenly let go and began to laugh, and went on laughing until tears streamed down her wrinkles to her chin. "My husband had that problem," she said. "And I never knew what to do. He used to shout at me when it happened, as if it were my fault. The bastard." Omm Kasim had never heard Zahra swear before.

"A pity you didn't write to Dr. Adil about his problem," Omm Kasim giggled. Then she paused, "And maybe I ought to write to him too. I'd like to write: 'Dear Dr. Adil, My husband's fat belly causes him all kinds of difficulties when he wants a fuck.'" Then she paused and added,

"And I'd finish my letter the same way that woman did. What does it say there? Oh, yes: 'Please, Dr. Adil, tell me what can I do to help? Signed, A Faithful Wife.'"

Then, Zahra began an imaginary letter of her own, "'Dear Dr. Adil, What is a good wife to do when her husband gets old, and his breath smells . . .'"

"'and his armpits stink,'" Omm Kasim interrupted,

"'and his feet smell,'" Zahra continued,

"'and when he makes love like a tortoise with grunts and squeaks?'"

When they finally stopped laughing, Omm Kasim said, "But it's not his lovemaking that bothers me. What is much worse is that he's lost his nerve. They shout at him and then he lets them shout at me." Then she paused, "He's really no better than a limp penis."

"Worse perhaps," Zahra said. "Mine had a limp penis, but at least he was a man of character."

After that famous afternoon, Omm Kasim really put her mind to saving money. She was proud that she'd discovered two different ways of doing it.

First, she began to shop at the Friday Market near the shrine of Ibn Arabi at Mouhiaddin. She hadn't bothered to go that far since the time when she'd heard some boys whispering that the saint's feet stuck out of his tomb and she'd wanted to see for herself. They didn't, of course, and she'd been angry at the peasants and the bawling of their donkeys and the puddles of dirty water in the streets where the stall holders had tried to settle the dust. This time she cared only that the vegetables were a little cheaper and she could find prickly pear fruits for less than a lira each.

The first time she returned home, hunched and sweaty, with her fingers deeply ribbed by the plastic handles of her shopping bags, Kasim had shouted, "You foolish woman, the house is filthy. I order you to stay home and clean it."

She'd stopped arguing with Kasim, but she dared not be too silent or it would provoke him further, so she screamed back, "Have some respect for me. I've been shopping for your lunch."

The following Friday she slipped past his corpulent, snoring body on the divan in the hall and stopped at Zahra's first. From then on they went together and carried things back and stored some of them at Zahra's. Zahra enjoyed the Friday Market, and loved the cheese sold by the Bedouin women who stood tall and tattooed between the canopied stalls.

One Friday, Omm Kasim watched when Zahra approached a grubby child playing with a small tortoise next to a pile of melons. Zahra bargained with the child and bought the creature for an extravagant four lira and put it in one of her plastic bags. Once home, she climbed the narrow stairs and placed the tortoise in the center of her little garden.

"It will bring good luck," she said.

Omm Kasim nodded and smiled at Zahra. Then she grinned, "We should call it Abu Kasim," and Zahra agreed with a hoot of laughter. "And from now on," Omm Kasim said, "please call me Samira, it is my own real name."

Omm Kasim's second plan for saving money was inspired by the chicken joke that Zahra, of all people, had told her. "Omm Kasim, have you heard what happened to the peasant who wanted to sell his chickens at the Friday Market? No? Well, at the first roadblock, one of the guards asked, 'What's in your truck?' And when the peasant answered, 'Chickens,' the guard demanded to know what the chickens ate. The poor peasant was terrified and answered, 'Why the best food, of course.' But it was the wrong answer, and the guard shouted, 'You can't give them the best food when so many people are hungry,' and he beat the peasant and confiscated all his chickens.

"Of course, what did he expect?" Omm Kasim asked dismissively. She was nonplused when Zahra said, "Shush and listen."

"So," Zahra continued, "the next time the peasant was quizzed at a roadblock, he had the cunning to answer, 'My chickens survive on the poorest food.' But the guard shouted, 'You can't do that or you'll poison people,' and again he confiscated the chickens and this time he threw the peasant in jail."

"Ummm," said Omm Kasim, remembering the verve with which Anwar told jokes.

"By the third time," Zahra resumed, "the peasant had learned a thing or two. When the guard asked what the chickens ate, he replied, 'Oh, I just give them pocket money and they buy their own food.' This time," Zahra said with a flourish, "the guard was so impressed, he let the peasant pass and take his chickens to the Friday Market."

Omm Kasim laughed dutifully, then with delight. She was glad Zahra had started to tell jokes. Moreover, between rationing and the idea of pocket money, Omm Kasim devised her second savings plan.

If her family wanted *fatet magdus*—or chicken—they could eat in a restaurant or look for it on the black market. But from her, from now on, they would only get the bare essentials. But, of course, Omm Kasim defined the bare essentials very carefully so that they would not riot, or even notice what they were missing.

She continued to make their coffee for breakfast. That couldn't be altered. But lunch was different. On Fridays Bashar and Faiz and the slut always expected to eat *ful*, so why not have beans and bread other lunchtimes as well? Since Kasim wanted only hamburgers, why not add soft bread crumbs to the ground beef? One day she even tried *hummus* as a filler, but Kasim swore and said she'd bought bad meat. It was only some time later that she found she could make the meat go further by simply adding mashed potato.

Abu Kasim was more difficult to please. He believed food was as much as love. He liked lots of different dishes on the table and loved to comment scientifically about why beans and cracked wheat must be eaten together, and why tomato sauce should never be served with yogurt. But after her success with the hamburgers, she realized that she could add rice or bulgur to virtually anything to make it last day after day. Then, some time later, Omm Kasim's savings plan had another, unexpected effect. She found, without really noticing it happen, that she had learned to cut the vegetables into bigger, and yet bigger, pieces. And one day she astonished herself by vowing that she would never, ever, again take the trouble to chop parsley for *tabouli*.

Over the following months, the lunch menus became more and more sparse. But they were so used to shouting at her, they didn't seem to notice that they now had more to shout about.

Then one day Omm Kasim exchanged the coins in her purse for bills. But as she grew richer, she grew more worried. She knew Kasim and Bashar often looked in her handbag and stole coins for themselves. She also knew that the slut sometimes went through her things, though whether from boredom or malice, she didn't know. She decided it would be better to leave the money with Zahra.

"Ah, my mother-in-law loves me." It was winter when Anwar next popped his head round the front door and invited himself to lunch. After the meal, when the rest of them, disgruntled by his good humor, had taken themselves off, Omm Kasim invited him to share a pot of tea.

"Anwar, I need your help," she said urgently. "One of our neighbors has no one at all. She comes to us every night to watch television and we're not even kin. I have made a vow—but you must never tell anyone—that I will help her."

Anwar was abashed by Omm Kasim, the unexpected saint.

"I've put some money aside, enough I think for a small television. Could you see if you can find one, a cheap one, secondhand?"

"Of course. I'll see what I can find." As she'd hoped, he was so clearly astonished by her request that he couldn't refuse.

"Oh, thank you. God bless you. Now come. Quietly. I'll show you her house. And if—when?" she looked at him expectantly, "when you find the right set, could you take it straight there and get it working?"

Zahra was dumbstruck when several weeks later Anwar and a black-and-white television arrived at her front door. Then, when Omm Kasim arrived—Zahra had never had two visitors in the little house at the same time—the three of them shared Hourani jokes and glasses of sweet mint tea, while Anwar sorted out the wires at the back of the set, adjusted the antenna and, with evident pleasure, tuned in the picture.

"It should be fine," he said, looking at the two beaming old women, "and if there are any problems you must tell me and I'll come and sort things out."

The day's broadcasting began midafternoon. Omm Kasim and Zahra took up places side-by-side on the divan and were so enchanted by the sound and images which filled the room that it hardly mattered that they were watching the opening religious program and a turbaned sheik droning verses of the Koran.

And when the children's programs began, they laughed delightedly at the antics of Majid, the cartoon Pinocchio. Omm Kasim even put her hand to her nose and rather wondered if she should find a mirror. That evening, when Zahra failed to arrive at her usual time, Omm Kasim said quietly to Abu Kasim, "Zahra may be ill. I think I should go and see," and she slipped on her overcoat and scarf, and walked down to the tiny house with the blue light flickering from the window.

TRUE LOVE

Sahar was driving her husband's elderly Citröen with a verve that would have better suited a snappy new BMW. Now, *she* is beautiful, Ahmed thought. Her face was so precisely delicate that it made you expect gentle, downcast eyes. But they weren't. They were almost black, and so deep they glowed with reflected light like animal eyes in the dark. Sahar's eyes belied her patterned head scarf and pale gray overcoat which were, she said, an easy way to please her husband.

Ahmed glanced again at his sister. She was thriving on this business of finding him a bride. Then, remembering the reason why they were speeding toward Malky in

the late morning heat, Ahmed choked at the absurdity of
it all. He tried to straighten his legs to reclaim some
sense of dignity, but he was too tall for the car and could
barely separate his knees from his chin.

"So tell me where we're going this time?" Ahmed
made a face, trying to remember how this whole business
had started. Sahar, ever the big sister, gave him a baleful
look. "To see a girl who's just finished at the American
School and is very beautiful."

"Thanks, Sahar. That tells me a lot." As far as he
could remember, she'd described all the young women
they'd visited in exactly the same way. He was too old for
this game and he wondered why he'd volunteered to sit
on the torturer's spike.

They were all nymphets who either thought marriage was all there was to life, or that a good catch was
something you beheaded and hung on the wall. Quick-
ened by resentment, he turned on Sahar. "So, how did
you find this one?" he asked, then regretted his sneer.

"Umm, let me see . . . ," Sahar paused as if she spent
all her time cruising Damascus for young women. "I first
saw her at that new ice cream parlor opposite the Apollo.
She was with three other girls, eating a sundae at one of
the corner tables. She was so shiny compared with the
others and I liked her hair. It reminded me of mama's.

"She was wearing a wonderful blouse, half lace, half
lurex, and still demure. So I went over and admired the
blouse. I asked her where it was from, told her I had a
daughter just starting high school, mentioned who we
were and asked her her name, of course. It was the only
polite thing to do."

In spite of the whir of the traffic at the big roundabout at the bottom of Malky, Sahar risked looking over
at Ahmed, before adding with a grin, "A woman who
wears a head scarf and frumpy overcoat can do almost
anything, you know."

"Anyway, she's clever and from a good family. With
English from the American School, and someone told me
that she'd been staying with a brother in Paris in the

summers to learn some French. So the basic bits are all right, aren't they?"

"Sahar, just shut up, will you?" Sahar's eagerness to matchmake made him worry that she would take the whole thing too far. That she'd end up cheering him on from behind the bedroom curtains on his wedding night. Whenever that would be.

"You shut up," Sahar replied, her good humor unimpaired. "And just think for a moment how she must be feeling right now. Her name is Nada, by the way. And also by the way, your complaints are becoming tedious. Whatever you say, you're not an animal being hauled off to the Souq el Bedawi. We'll get straight to the point and if the two of you don't care for each other, that's it. Everybody's civil from beginning to end, no one gets hurt, and there's no messing about."

Ahmed grunted. At least it was straightforward. Though he felt like a fool and wondered if that was why Sahar found this business so much fun.

"You ought to consider yourself fortunate to have a loving sister to do the groundwork for you." She gleamed a smile at him, "If you hadn't spent so much time in London, you'd know this system can work. And anyway you didn't meet the right person there, did you?"

Sahar had never given him any quarter, so why should he expect it now? Then suddenly, a memory of Caroline seared through him. He grabbed for a cigarette and lit it quickly to stop the hurt spreading. He knew it had been his problem, not Caroline's. She'd been terrific, but so lively he couldn't relax. "Tight-ass," she'd say, and that's what it felt like, and still felt like, if he were honest.

But it wasn't just the two of them or they might have sorted things out. There was also Caroline's visit to Damascus when he'd stayed behind to finish the thesis which had refused to be written earlier. The family had found her delightful, of course, and even asked her to stay on for an extra week. But the fiction they adopted was that he and Caroline were just good friends. It was a story they weren't prepared to alter, however much they liked her.

The "just good friends" said it all, considering how the family had behaved the year before. It had slipped out, during one of mama's weekly phone calls, that he'd been seeing something of Samir's sister. He still wanted to kick himself for having mentioned it. Not only had mama started making wedding noises, but papa had phoned again the same night. To tell him about the new electronics businesses coming to Syria and the nice flat he was thinking of buying in Mezze.

So here he was letting Sahar drive him to the fifth— or was it the sixth?—of these rendezvous. Even now he could hardly remember the others. No, not true. The first one did stick in his mind. Perhaps his embarrassment made it memorable, because it certainly wasn't the girl. She'd been the tall one. Ahmed shut his eyes and could see her dark blue dress and the matronly way she'd moved through a drawing room fusty with inlaid furniture. "Yes," she'd said, "I do like reading. Ghada al-Samman's stories are my favorites," and that had been it as far as he was concerned.

"Mild and ordinary," had been Sahar's verdict when she got back into the car. It was then that Sahar had confessed, "the woman I want for you will have plenty of character, but is still open, and fun, and willing to learn."

Ahmed wasn't immune to the flattery implicit in the standards Sahar had set for herself as a matchmaker. And, over the last couple of weeks, he had become increasingly amused by her research and development approach to choosing a wife: design specifications, limits of tolerance, a clear idea of the marketing package and the product competition. It had made him think he should have specialized in robotics rather than computer hardware. Then another treacherous Caroline-thought crept into his head, making his insides shrink and ache horribly. He could imagine how wickedly funny she'd be if she knew about all this. And sympathetic, he had to admit. She always seemed to know what he was thinking no matter how confused he felt. It was Caroline who'd backed off, probably because she understood him too well.

The ache only retreated when he lit up another cigarette. As a kind of aversion therapy, he forced himself to remember the second visit. He had to think hard, until he remembered that the second girl was the one Sahar had whispered was inelegant, *musharshara*, the moment the girl had gone to make them coffee.

Of course Sahar had done her homework: the girl was pretty, and no doubt clever, and she was from an old Damascene family. But the tricky bit about old families, Ahmed was beginning to realize, is that they are often very, very big. And even Sahar couldn't always sort out all the cousins and cousins of cousins, or the ones she thought had the right sort of money and breeding from the rest who'd be hoping their family name would hide genteel poverty or money which was a bit too new.

"Cheap and trashy," Sahar had sniffed when they got back to the car.

"How can you be so sure?" Though he had to admit the girl was brittle and lacked Sahar's, and Caroline's, easy charm.

"You mean you didn't see her eyes?" Sahar was incredulous. "They were like green glass beads stuck in the head of a porcelain tiger. Those contact lenses are fashionable now. I'll bet she got a pair just for you. But she is a prowler. An opportunist, a real *harbouah*. Not up to you at all."

Ahmed had never heard of green contacts before and he wondered how his staid sister knew about such things, and how she could be so certain about her own good taste. Still, what's pleasing about Sahar, Ahmed thought, is that she's never defensive about her matchmaking. Indeed, he suspected she enjoyed the risk of arranging a meeting when there wasn't quite enough information to make it predictable. He also suspected she didn't mind that he was discomfited on the way. She's a bit like Caroline, expecting him to learn from his unease. Sahar saw these marriage visits as a game they

could only win and he was amazed by her endless curiosity. If she made a mistake, as with tiger-eyes, she'd just
shrug and say, 'A lucky escape.' He was disposed to trust
her. She understood how family differences can make for
a miserable marriage. It was a lesson she'd learned the
hardest way.

Sahar's husband had looked all right at first: land,
money, a graduate degree from the States, but what
they'd all ignored was that his family was as deeply conservative as theirs was liberal. Suddenly, Ahmed realized
he was going through this marriage charade to please his
sister and he was shocked at himself.

"What did you say this one's name was?" he asked
peevishly.

"Haven't I said already? Her name is Nada. Lovely,
isn't it?" Sahar wrinkled her nose. "But I guess I would
think that." She played with the literal meanings of
the names: "Sahar-'dawn' would like the idea of Nada-
'morning dew.'" She laughed at herself, then got back to
the business at hand. "They've got a lot more money than
papa, so don't get your hopes up too high. Anyway, let's
just see. You've got things going for you: you're handsome," she said, and winked at him flirtatiously, and he
knew, because she'd told him before, that thirty-three is
young if you have a house and job in London.

Ahmed was grateful for Sahar's loyalty, though he
wasn't the least bit sure he'd pass muster if she were
working for the opposition. Doubt crept up on him like
the fluttering of a mouse near his heart and, to banish it,
he forced himself to remember the next two women
they'd visited. He discovered he couldn't recall the third
one at all, but he did remember the fourth and how he'd
been furious to learn that it wasn't only Sahar who'd
helped to make the choice.

He'd been so angry when she'd explained his
brother's contribution as if it were the most normal thing
in the world. As if playing the amateur photographer at
other people's weddings and snapping pictures of young
women he reckoned were beautiful enough to be Ahmed's

bride was a perfectly natural thing to do. Still, he couldn't make up his mind about the balance between innocence and lechery in his brother's photography. It made him wonder, yet again, why he'd given in to the idea of marrying someone from Damascus. The whole business was objectionable, and it seemed more and more likely that his whole family would fetch up in the bridal suite: Sahar behind the curtains, his brother ready to leap out of a cupboard like a paparazzo and his mother wringing her hands offstage. The fourth young woman, whoever she'd been, hadn't stood a chance after he'd heard how she'd been talent-spotted.

They were heading up Malky Boulevard when Sahar interrupted Ahmed's wedding nightmare. "Ahmed, you do know that it's a real bonus you've not been married before. People will think you've kept yourself pure for the right Damascene girl."

Ahmed looked up the long, wide street, shimmering pale in the late morning heat, then out at the Asad Library. In spite of himself, he considered the library the best modern building in Damascus.

"Of course, we know better than that, but it does help," Sahar added, smiling ruefully at her brother. Sahar had been Caroline's main supporter last summer. And she'd been devastated when Caroline had decided it wouldn't work. Sahar had kept in touch with Caroline, which, though it made him feel bad, was more than he could say. It was then too that he'd realized how much his big sister hated these marriage games. She probably hated them more than anyone else he knew.

So what in the hell are we doing now? Because he couldn't disentangle his anger from some shrugging sense of the ridiculous, he slipped another Lucky Strike out of the pack on the dashboard. "Don't light up another one," Sahar admonished, but he excused her sharpness when she added, "Look we're almost there. The house is supposed to be somewhere here behind the Indian Embassy."

The entrance hall to the apartment block was marbled and very clean. The lift worked and the terrace flat promised a breathtaking view over Damascus to the green haze of the oasis beyond. Girl Number Five's mother opened the door; she was young-looking and managed to make Ahmed feel surprisingly normal. He even had time to notice the white walls and white leather furniture. These could have worked against the mother's warmth, but they didn't. Perhaps it was the large oil painting, rich in reds against a twilight blue, which offset the austerity of the room. Or perhaps it was Nada's mother herself. He could see she had already made Sahar feel at home.

Then, after only a few minutes, the girl teased into the room. She'd chosen to wear the lace and lurex blouse again. In doing so, she blew any pretense that this was just an ordinary social visit straight out into the oasis. Sahar was clearly taken aback, but he was amused at her audacity. Nada—or at least her blouse—cut through the inevitable insincerities. This time even the care required to sip coffee might be a little less painful.

"The view is marvelous," Sahar commented, clearly eager to move them beyond the question of the blouse.

"Yes, it's lovely," Nada's mother joined in, "particularly when the air is clear."

Then Nada, who was standing near the wide glass doors to the balcony, exclaimed, "Do you see that flock of pigeons just turning out of the sun? I don't know how it happens but if you count them there are always exactly fourteen birds flying together. Isn't that strange?"

"Ummm," murmured Sahar, and Ahmed could see that she was now intrigued by both the girl, and the pigeons. When it was time for coffee, Nada again did something unexpected. "I hope you don't mind, but I had to go down to Salahhiye this morning, so I brought back some chocolate croissants from Moka. I thought they'd be lovely with café au lait."

"That sounds great," Ahmed said. However strong the tiny cups of Arab coffee, there was never enough caffeine to speed him through these visits. Then he glanced at Sahar and could see her mouth pursed and censoring.

He guessed she was trying to work out how much of the girl's confidence came from being rich and spoiled.

"What do you want to do, now that you've finished school?" Ahmed asked, cringing in anticipation of the obvious answer, even if it wasn't said openly.

"I'm not really sure. I've come to the end of the music I can do at the Academy and I'd like to do more." Then she laughed at the hint of admiration which must have crept across his face. "Oh, I wish I were good enough to perform, but I'm not. But I'd like to teach piano. Here, all I'd probably ever get to do is teach *solfege* to miserable kids with ambitious parents."

When she said this Ahmed remembered when Hala, his younger sister, had become a *solfege* dropout at the age of eight. The memory suddenly made him hurt again. Enthusiastic Hala, forced to do sight-singing for an entire year. She wasn't so much a lark ascending as plummeting headfirst to earth. And then there was Caroline, who played beautifully and always included him in her music.

"What kind of music do you like?" he asked, suddenly registering that Nada was stunning. Her honeyed hazel eyes matched her hair, and were very direct.

"Almost everything, really. 'Catholic taste' is what one says in English, I think. One of my brothers is a music man, and he's just introduced me to Keith Jarrett. Do you know his music?"

Ahmed nodded, then grinned, "You'll be able to guess my age, if I tell you I was at the Cologne concerts in 1975."

"Oh, lucky you. Like being at Woodstock, or the Horowitz concert in Moscow. I've just been trying to work through the music from Cologne."

"But I thought the whole point was improvisation?"

"Do you play the piano too?"

"No, but I like to listen."

"Oh, pity. Anyway, you're right. He transcribed it himself. It's hard, but I'll get there in the end."

Then she paused. "Well, you asked me what I want to do. I guess the short answer is I want to find a way to do some more music, and a teaching diploma, in either France or England." Then she paused again, "And, as I'm sure you'll understand, I'm not going to have to marry to manage that." It was said with such matter-of-factness that Ahmed felt rebuffed for just being there. Then another Caroline-thought skipped through his head: well, at least I know enough not to take this personally.

"I'm sorry," he said. "This whole business is embarrassing, isn't it?" Then he turned to Sahar. "Even you know it's mad, sister of mine." Then to Nada he added, "I think the main reason we're here is because it keeps Sahar alive and out of the house." He'd meant it to be playful, but from Sahar's sharp intake of breath he knew she thought he was mocking her. Nada looked at him intently and he wondered, abashed, whether she worked like a truth drug on other people as well.

The midday electricity cut had started by the time they left. Ahmed and Sahar walked down the stairs in a prudent silence, knowing how unpredictable the acoustics of a stairwell could be. When they finally reached the car, Ahmed said lightly, "Do you think a fair test of affluence is the amount of daylight which reaches the stairs?"

"I was also thinking about their wealth . . . ," Sahar said, but Ahmed interrupted.

"Well, she was a surprise after all the others." This time he left no time for Sahar to reply. "I liked her. Probably because she thinks as little of these introductions as I do." Sahar edged the car into the traffic at the Malky roundabout and back into the conversation. "Yes, it's certainly rare, that mixture of confidence and sincerity."

"Oh Sahar, stop being so bloody judicious. She looks great, she's sharp and honest, and she's a Keith Jarrett fan. She's the only one of your young women I'd ever want to see again, and yet she's thrown out the only pretext I have. Sahar, this marriage business stinks."

The lights at the pedestrian crossing at Tishreen Park turned red, and they watched a slender young man in a dusty *jellabiyya* carry a tousle-headed child across the street on his shoulder. "Ahmed, you've been away from Damascus too long. You haven't been treated badly. And, she did ask if you'd like to come to the concert on Thursday."

"The concert on Thursday. What you mean is the End of Term Recital at the Music Academy! Come on, Sahar, I'm thirty-three, not thirteen."

"Ahmed, you really don't understand," Sahar said testily. "First, how would you ever meet anyone like Nada except through family connections. Well, that's what we've done; we've started making connections. And second, a young woman like Nada doesn't go out alone with a man—however, nice he is—unless they're already engaged."

"But Sahar . . ."

"Ahmed, shut up and listen. People don't date here, at least not our sort of people. And, by the way, I'm sorry if you really are doing this just to keep me busy. But," she paused and shot him a challenging look, "if that's true, then the next step is easy. I'd appreciate the chance to get out, even if I have to sit like an old crow of a chaperone. So let's go to the concert. What else can I say?" He nodded, ashamed that he'd put her on the spot.

On Thursday evening in the foyer of the Arab Theater on Firdows, Ahmed realized he'd forgotten how rarely Damascenes get together and he could feel the rush of excitement in the chattering crowd. At last they found Nada's mother and then quickly found seats in the large auditorium. All around them animated groups of young women giggled and preened, and waved greetings to each other across the hall, while their parents nodded and rose to embrace close friends. Sahar and Nada's mother enjoyed the scene, comparing notes, laughing at how everyone was trying to upstage everyone else. It took a long time for the audience to settle in and the concert to begin.

Sitting next to Sahar, Ahmed found it easy to share her delight at the children's pieces. And he shared her

amused sympathy for the quartet whose progress
through a Haydn slow movement became increasingly
tentative as the cellist, who'd forgotten his spike-holder,
wrestled to keep his instrument from scooting under the
music stand. The clarinetist, a cousin of Nada's, was very
good. Along with the bright flow of his music, a Caroline-
thought slipped into Ahmed's head. He was grateful, and
relieved, to think that Caroline too would have enjoyed
the evening.

Then, finally, Nada came on to play the first movement of the Waldstein Sonata. Her gown was cerise, as
luscious as a cherry, and he couldn't think of anything
but the way the dress outlined the shape of her breasts.
He was pleased the Beethoven was so strenuous and he
guessed, from the applause at the end, that she must
have played well.

Later Nada returned again to the stage, this time
accompanied by a little girl whose white socks and dress
made her look like an angel. Nada adjusted the height of
the chairs and they began to play a simple piece from the
Dolly Suite. Ahmed saw Nada's calm spread round the
child. Nada, he decided, was altogether lovely.

The next week there was a second concert, the last
that members of the Music Academy would give in the
old building. This time the crowd was smaller, and more
stylish, and he considered how silly he must look, sitting
side by side with Nada, with Sahar and Nada's mother
gossiping next to them. But their good spirits were con-
tagious, and joking with Nada was too much fun to be
spoiled by being pompous. By being tight-assed, as Caroline would say.

During the following month, he was surprised by
how often he and Nada managed to be together. They had
a fierce badminton match at a picnic her parents had organized for their friends. That was when Sahar had
charmed Nada's father and persuaded him to play dou-
bles until they'd collapsed in laughter. And they'd had a
chance to dance together at a wedding party at the Oriental Club for a couple whose families belonged to the

same circles as their own. Almost every day they sipped lemonade at the Sheraton pool where Nada came with one of her brothers. Each time she looked away, he would do a recount of her freckles. And almost every time, she'd catch him staring at her legs and laugh at him and he'd feel absolutely great.

"Sahar, what am I going to do?" Ahmed asked one morning when he'd come specially to see his sister. "I've got to get back to London, but I really don't want to leave. Or, let me be honest, I don't want to leave because of Nada."

"Have you talked to her about how you feel?" Ahmed nodded.

"And what does she say?"

"We'd like to become engaged. And get married next summer, maybe in June. Do you think it will work? Do you think her family will agree?"

Sahar paused for a long time, "Who can tell whether a marriage will work, but I hope so, for both your sakes." Then she smiled, "And, yes, I think her family will agree, otherwise you'd never have seen as much of her as you have. But there will be a lot to sort out before they'll be happy. They're careful and she's the only daughter."

"Sahar, will you help? It's important. In fact, it was almost love at first sight."

"Yes, funny how it happens," Sahar mused, a guileless look on her face. Then her black eyes sparked and she added, "Of course, I'll help. I'll help both of us. What do you think I've been doing all this time?"

JELLYFISH

Leila listened to the voice. You can only die if God allows you to. It was stentorian, insistent. It was telling her she must go forward with measured steps, and that there could be no bending, or shuffling, that she mustn't falter, should never pause or look sideways for a glimpse of other choices.

Stop, you bloody noise, Stop. She gulped and sucked in the sea air. Do you think I want to die? Do you? It's a sin to think that. She shouted at the sound which pressed inside her head. Her skin pulled tight, and anguish seared her spine, then a whirlpool of grief dragged her down to an airless deep so dense it turned the sunlight gray.

Then, as suddenly as it had come, the voice, and the
pain, left and her body floated back up to the light.
Beached and dizzy, Leila sat vacant, looking out to sea.
But as feeling returned, she remembered she wasn't
alone, that there were others who might have seen.

She looked across the heat-swept beach to the other
women lazing under the faded awning. They were just
like her, were her best friends, sharing a holiday in Tartus. She began the litany of self-congratulation they often
sang to each other: to beauty and sophistication and good
Damascene families. Leila's mouth went dry. Well, almost
like her, except at thirty they'd found husbands, had tiny
children and were proud of what they'd done.

Watching herself in the mirror of this unforgiving
audience, she bent her knees and curled languidly onto
her hip, balancing easily on the fulcrum of her left elbow.
She composed her face and lifted her head as precisely as
if two taut metal strings were guiding the movement
from the tops of her ears. Then brushing her thigh, she
let the coconut oil trail down the waxed smoothness of
her leg before flicking the sand from the tips of her toes
which shone with silver polish. Leila was pleased: a
tableau of feminine beauty for Georges.

When her portrait of Georges was in focus, she ex-
amined it critically and made him a bit taller and added
glints of red to his hair. If only she'd met him sooner. As
she sighed, Georges became a shadow, and a pain, so
deep it must have come from another dimension, spread
through her body in waves.

Leila looked again at her friends, imagining what
they were saying, could even hear them saying it.

Leila looks happy.

But it's very hot. Is she all right?

She's fine. She's just sitting there to get a darker tan.

Not even Leila's that vain. She offered to look after
the boys.

That's generous of her. But what does she know
about children?

Of course it wasn't fair. Was fair. Was maybe partly
true. As if they cared about the three toddlers playing at

her feet. She wondered why she had offered to look after them, then let the thought drift away. In any case, she was here: here to prevent the little boys from falling face-forward in the puddles round their moated sand castle; here to keep them from straying down the beach or walking out into the waves which were beginning to roll with late morning urgency. She was here because their mothers wished that all small children would play on a storybook beach where there are no tears, or sand fleas, or demands for popcorn, a can of cold *mandolin* and endless attention.

Suddenly the sun-soaked morning was disturbed. The water sprites on the diving platform began to abandon the wobbling boards and swim ashore. Leila could hear the young men shouting. "Jellyfish! Lots of them. Out of the water. Everyone out of the water." Leila smiled. For all their bravado, the would-be pinups soon retreated to the shore themselves. There was no scope for heroism with jellyfish: everyone knew a full-frontal encounter could hospitalize, while the merest brush left a dark stain which ached with venom for days.

"Damn them," Leila cursed the jellyfish. Though it wasn't because she wanted to swim. Or rather, she would love to swim, but you had to be confident and young to cavort on a public beach. No, she was far too old for that, or, at least, they would think it indelicate, or desperate, at thirty-three.

She took a deep breath, and looked again at the laughing young men and women who were now settling themselves on the sand. When some of the lads began to kick a football wildly up and down the beach, Leila swore at their thoughtlessness and fiercely called her toddlers back to her side.

She could hear them again.

Youth hurts, doesn't it, Leila?

Is that what's upset her?

Perhaps it's the filth. Aren't jellyfish spawned in pollution? The pollution which is killing the Mediterranean Sea.

Whose pollution? Theirs or ours? a voice said, as a huge rusty cargo ship wallowed between the sea and sky.

No, it's not the foul jellyfish, it's that the youngest and brightest have been forced off their raft and onto the beach, where even near-sighted Leila can see them clearly. Isn't that it, Leila?

Leila didn't know how the voices had started, but they stopped when she saw that some of the lads had trapped one of the cloudy white jellyfish in a pool of dirty water. The little children had seen them too and dashed over to join the circle of young men peering at the pulsating creature. With the first burst of energy she'd invested in the morning, Leila swooped down on her toddlers and, as she danced them back to the sand castle, the mother of one of the little boys waved her a casual thanks.

So why do they have children? And how dare they flaunt them? A mocking round began in her head: our - children - come - after - sex - with - husbands - we've - caught - and - married. The chant got louder with each repetition.

Shut up, Leila cried, trying to drown the blare of the accompanying processional music, the pomp of the wedding parade, and the sight of the glittering guests. She only rid herself of the vision when she diminished the bride and groom. Sneering at their self-satisfaction, she stuck their feet in the icing on the top of the cake.

Or perhaps the scene had vanished when she'd looked down at the toddlers squatting on fat legs, peering over their round bellies to poke holes in the castle walls.

That's better. Look at the children. They don't watch, or judge. Perhaps that's why she'd volunteered to look after them, to give up her time for an hour or two. They didn't want to do it. They saw it as a chore, resented them, their own children. They give them life and say they love them. But they don't. What they love is matronly righteousness.

Georges loves children, she thought, and lifted her head to stare insolently at her judges, who lay spread and fleshy on the dark green towels from holiday chalets. The deliberate curves of their cosseted bodies were

marked with the shadows of creases which turned the
women into a single, barely breathing, form. Their pale,
recumbent figures were rounded into a featureless mass.
Jellyfish, Leila thought and she felt special for Georges.

Leila is different away from Damascus.

Yes, calmer, it seems to me.

This week is doing her good.

Is it? I don't think so, Leila answered back. And as
the weight of her anger threatened to mold her into the
sand, she felt her body begin to rock, to sway.

One of the little boys aimed a gleeful arch of pee into
the moat of the sand castle. "Stop that!" Leila shouted, so
loudly that both she and the toddler jumped. "Stop that!
It's 'ayb, it's very naughty."

Strident Leila. Crazy Leila.

That's what they'll say. And they'll let my mother
know.

Leila reached out for her fear and steadied herself.
How dare they gossip? If I cry, they'll think I've had an
affair. But she knew she must wrap her anger in a damp
towel to let it cool slowly. If I'm upset, it will show on my
skin. I'll come out in spots, get premature wrinkles, a
corduroy mouth.

She cooled her rage with her beauty care. Georges
thinks I'm lovely. Leila tried to decide whether he had
brown eyes or blue. Then she allowed herself to look down
at her shapely nose. She didn't dare do it often—her eyes
might stick, or someone might see her cross-eyed and notice her nose was new. So she snatched a glance at the
half-veiled darkness, shadowed in one eye, translucent to
the other. Then she squinted and winked and reversed the
shadow, and the translucence. Georges thinks I'm lovely.

"Auntie Leila?" the little boy she'd shouted at looked
up at her. "What are you doing?"

She started, then brushed her hair away from her
face. "Nothing. A grain of sand in my eye."

Bored by her reply, the child walked off dragging a
plastic spade. But what if they saw? They would laugh,
and mock her, and chase Georges out of her head.

Do you remember her nose?

She waited too long to have it done.

Sickle-nosed Leila. Perhaps that's why she never married.

But she had many suitors. Once she was even engaged.

But no one was perfect, none good enough.

There'll be someone soon.

No, she's too bitter, no one will want her.

She's not as strong as she'd have us believe.

Leila was frightened by the incalculable scope of their words. Please, let me alone, she cried.

But how do you know what we're saying?

Because that's the way gossip works.

Are you sure? the baiting continued. Do you think others are like you? They say *enti mazambura*, you talk too much and are hungry for sex. So full of hurt that you meddle and trouble others.

Damn them. They're jealous. They hate me because I didn't sell myself like a sack of potatoes, because I didn't jump at the first man I saw.

From under the awning someone waved. Leila flashed her widest smile and waved back. Then she picked up one of the toddlers, hugged his squirming body, gave him an extravagant kiss and began to swing him above her head. The little boy grumped, kicked out at Leila and started to cry. The exquisite watching faces were satisfied she was doing her job. Leila let the child slip back down to the sand and picked up a dream child of Georges's instead.

The waves grew longer and larger and began churning up the sand. The air became hazy and refracted the brown of the sea in the sky. Where were the Mediterranean storms that sent the waves rolling in at midday? Or was it storms at all? No, more likely, the insufferable scorching beyond Tartus and the mountains out toward the desert. Maybe that's why people are hard and harsh?

Stop it, Leila cried. That makes no sense of the kindness of spring, or the soft whiteness of peoples' skins.

Look at me, making myself leathery. It's people and gossip which makes us tough, not the land.

Than a voice, gruff with disapproval, chided her self-pity: Leila sits by the edge of the water daring the waves to suck her down and pull her into the sea.

No, that's not it. That's far more brave than the truth. I'm here to help build a sand castle—a Qalat el Hosn—from the yellow sand of Tartus. But the towers in her mind repelled this lie and despair tightened her face. Leila, let go. Stop knowing so much. But she couldn't let go. What she wanted, as strong as her body could feel, was to order the words and tidy them into rings of iron filings.

That much control? No, not control. Calm. Georges was calm. Calm in the eye of the storm. Like the pilgrims in Mecca. The pilgrims who pray in great circles toward the Kaba, the magnet, the center of the world.

Blasphemer, a fierce, deep voice said.

What made her think of Mecca? It can only be God's knowing.

Of course, people look at young women. There are always the eyes of the watchers, the friends and the judges who see and condemn—never praise, never praise—and tell others all that they know. A pious Leila suddenly cried, If I must be watched, let it be by God alone.

Her prayer was interrupted by the shouts of young men who'd trapped more jellyfish in a bucket and were carrying them toward the pool. Once there, they pounded the creatures with stones. Water and pieces of stinging flesh showered the ghouls who'd gathered to enjoy the massacre and they ran away shrieking. Then the youths used sticks to poke the translucent flesh and when a sliver tore free, they waved it about on a stick.

Leila stood stock still watching the frenzied scene. It was a moment or two before she realized that her toddlers were among the audience, applauding the youths and risking the victims' venomous touch. For the second time, she rushed forward to pull the children to safety. This time none of their mothers saw.

Leila's anger burned. They want me to marry and have children. To vindicate their lives. Again she could feel words rushing dangerously round her head. Was she talking out loud, was she talking herself to death?

"You must learn to keep silent," her mother said. "Stop your chatter. People talk about the way you talk, you know. Learn to be silent," her mother had said.

Her mother spied on her these days, watching when she thought Leila was busy, or on the phone, or giving music lessons to Mohammed. Her mother looked at her sideways during lunch and afterward when she helped with the dishes. This watching, the pity—no, not pity—disapproval, dislike, disappointment. Leila hated it. Hated her mother. Hated her mother as much as her mother hated her. Leila, the daughter of great promise, had failed, could never now retrieve the time lost, could never start again.

What did I do wrong? Leila wanted to scream at her mother, to scream at the fat, halting woman with her rich dresses and her sharp eyes which flicked round any gathering, weighing up potential, measuring success, counting the money.

"Leila, hold your head high, like that little girl over there. Do you see the one who walks so beautifully? A real star, that one. Leila, hold your head high.

"Leila, those shoes, they don't flatter your legs. Wear the navy heels. They pinch your feet? Well, no matter, they are in better taste, you must see that.

"Leila, find a husband and marry. We're getting old, and who will look after you when we're gone? How will you manage alone?"

An ache rose through Leila's body to her mouth where it choked her and formed a gob of spit which she longed to spew over her mother's jutting bosom. Leila didn't spit—wished she could spit—but instead reached among the towels and the sun cream for the box of tissues with Love—yes, Love—written in Arabic script along its pastel length. Leila caught sight of the shadow of her new nose flattened and snubbed on the sand. Mothers raise daughters to hand them over to husbands. Mothers teach daughters to decorate their bodies with pain.

You'll never get free of her, will you?

Why should I want to get free? I'm intelligent, beautiful, look at me. Georges says I'm beautiful. What more could anyone want?

Her mother's answer erupted scalding into her head. "I'll only be happy when you're happily married."

You'll never be happy. Not even then.

"Leila, Papa's home from work." A swing upward, her short dress and white socks flying, a kiss on his scratchy cheek, then she was dropped like a stone in deep water. She struggled to the surface, to climb up his knees.

"Now Leila, don't disturb your father. Go and play in your room. Daughter, stop your pestering and go away."

Love—not love, not a father's love. I am the dresses he brings me from Rome. The dresses in my wardrobe, to be pressed and laid out, to be worn for an hour and returned to their cellophane, their hangers, and embalmed in lavender and the scent of cedar.

One of the toddlers squealed as the running edges of the waves came closer to the castle moat. When the next wave broke and slid in, it sucked over the sand, pushing debris and brown bubbles of foam before it. A tiny piece of poisonous flesh touched Leila's heel and she cried out. The little boys rushed over to inspect her foot, then giggled and fled away from the sea. Leila carried her towel back behind the castle walls.

Leila of too much promise, a refrain started pounding in her head. Clever Leila, too clever by half.

Dumb Leila, a voice laughed. Gullible Leila, who believes in romance, who believes in love at first sight. Your mother never taught you that. You taught yourself, with magazines and love stories, and teenage chatter. You believed in everything, in boyfriends and respect, in independence and wealth.

I can wait, you said, I'm young and beautiful. I can wait for a man who will love me for myself.

But you were wrong, Leila. You loved yourself too well.

She gave herself chances, but she couldn't take them.

She's mad, the voices hissed, she's mad and she's missed her life.

She's proud, too proud to see.

Love, they sniggered, she believes in love.

Leila wept at the chanting voices. No, I don't believe in love, I've stopped believing in love. Love is a label that hides whatever's there. But no, I won't agree to marry a man who is old and fat, or foolish. Or a man with children who comes for a nursemaid, a nanny. No.

A large wave crashed onto the sand and dribbled forward, pushing, drooling toward Leila's toes, threatening to catch her, to lick her manicured feet.

Sex. That's what they want. But Georges is different. Georges respects me and I respect him. We are secret companions, real friends. We are invisible, Georges and I.

No, they don't know about Georges. They can't know, can they? But we meet, of course we meet. How could you think that we don't? But carefully: in a restaurant he knows in Bab Tooma and in the room of his friend. Who? Elias. Yes, another Christian of course, whom I've never met, who doesn't know me. But no, I don't, do I? How can I? I'm Leila, the virgin. And Georges doesn't ask. Georges is a gentleman, and Georges is all mine.

The story moved in Leila's head, back and forth—no, not rocking—swinging. Swinging, up and away. Fast, push, and faster, swooping forward, swooping back, the whoosh of breeze in her hair, in her ears. Gather Georges in and let him protect you, then tuck in your legs and go higher and higher. Then fall back in safety and stretch out again, and again, and again.

Leila lay on the sand. Part of her held tight to her body and part of her soared—up and back—in arcs of hidden pleasure. And when she went higher, up to the point when the ropes jumped and dropped down—a spasm coiled out from inside her and she cried, then laughed out loud.

FRESH APRICOTS

Kasim smiled, then slouched and squeezed his heavy body under the steering wheel of the battered yellow Fiat. He liked it when this car turned up on his shift. This car, with its red plush interior, the strings of beads swinging from the visors and the decal of puckered lips blowing him a kiss from the dashboard.

As Kasim pulled out into the traffic, he switched on the headlights, then glanced through the rearview mirror. He smiled again, this time at the twin portraits of the President printed on the two sunshades that stretched down over the back window. Reversed, the portraits looked out, their eyes working like spotlights to

protect him from whatever might swoop down and catch
him unawares.

Almost immediately an old man hailed the taxi.
Three times what's on the meter, if Kasim would take
him up the Sednayya road. That's what the old devil of-
fered. It was a hell of a lot farther from the center than
Kasim wanted to go, but he could pick up the difference.
It wasn't too bad a start to the evening shift.

Driving up and out of Damascus, Kasim played the
executioner, watching how his headlights revealed men
walking along the gray slopes at the road's edge, then
plunged them back into darkness. Kasim also noticed the
clustered families and groups of heavy, scarved women
waiting with their bags and bundles near the bus shel-
ters. It amused him to think that one or two of these
characters would soon pay him for the privilege of riding
down to the city.

"We get off the main road here." Kasim's mood
turned sour as he turned the car to the left and his
anger increased as the old man peered out uncertainly
at the rows of raw concrete buildings. Most had hollow,
black holes for windows and piles of newly dug earth
round their foundations. Yet at intervals along the wide,
empty streets, there were other buildings in which every
window was brightly lit as if testifying to Damascus's
housing needs.

"What is the name of the building?" Kasim growled,
sullen, ratty at being out of town. But there was no one
on the street to ask until, finally, he stopped in the soli-
tary pool of noisy yellow light from a pressure lamp. The
vegetable seller's directions were also confused and
Kasim swore. He hated this blundering through the
nowhere places around Damascus.

Eventually, when he turned the taxi back toward the
Sednayya road, he snorted at the old man's generosity
and despised his uncertainty as he tottered off toward
what Kasim guessed would be a dubious welcome.

The corner was dark where the wide, unfinished
street finally met the main road. Kasim swore again. He
was farther out of Damascus than he'd meant to be

To console himself he shoved his precious Feruz tape into the machine and made a moue at the kissable lips on the dashboard. He almost missed the peasant-type in flared trousers and a crumpled shirt who was limping heavily as he tried to flag him down. I should think so too, Kasim said to himself; his was the only vehicle in sight.

"Damascus, please." The man's voice was smoother than Kasim had expected.

"Yeah, get in. But it'll cost you." Kasim checked in the mirror to be sure the guy understood. He could see a flick of hesitation in the man's glance before he said, "Yes, I can pay. Take me to El Jisr el Abiad, please."

The "please" was ingratiating. Kasim glanced again in the mirror. The guy was sitting tensed, upright, as if he didn't know how long the journey would take on a Thursday evening. Otherwise he looked alright, though older than Kasim had figured when he'd first seen the skinny figure reaching out toward his headlights from the murk at the side of the road.

He was staring into the darkness which pressed round the car. "I guess you don't make this journey often," Kasim ventured. He was no good at chatting up the punters. Whatever he said, it always came out slow and heavy, and anyway, they all knew—everyone knew—that his boss would ask if anything interesting had happened during the shift. No one wanted to be memorable.

"I guess you don't make this journey often," Kasim tried again. The second time the man looked a bit startled, then answered with none of the wariness Kasim was used to.

"No, I've never come this way before." Kasim waited, but the man was silent, preoccupied with the darkness outside.

"Our neighbors are from Sednayya, from the village, before it became fashionable."

"Is it fashionable?" the man asked.

"Yeah, it's posh." Envy greened Kasim's words, "Villas, weekend parties, and all that."

"Oh, I see," the man said, but clearly didn't, or perhaps saw only Kasim's resentment swinging violently like the beads on the visor as he took the badly cambered curve a bit too fast.

This guy was getting annoying. It was as if he wasn't all there. And he stank of chicken-shit, mildew, and disinfectant all mixed together. Maybe he works on one of the new factory farms, Kasim thought.

"What's your work?" he asked. He could see that the man didn't notice the intrusiveness of the question.

"I used to write . . ." he started. "I'm a teacher."

"Oh," said Kasim. That made sense of his careful accent, but less than no sense of his clothes. Usually it didn't take many clues for Kasim to slot people into a few basic categories, but this guy was a new type. Kasim was curious to know how he made his money, how he survived. Kasim was always interested in a scam.

"What do you teach? Mathematics?" That should be enough of a compliment to get anybody going.

"No, mostly reading," the man answered softly, "to men who didn't learn to read in school . . ."

"So why do they want to read?" Some of his friends envied him his high school diploma, but they were fools if they couldn't see the nowhere place it had got him.

"They read to keep themselves busy, to open up their world," the man said.

Kasim looked back sharply. What was all this drivel? And why wasn't he moaning, like all the other teachers, about low pay—not enough to keep a family—and forty-two kids running around a classroom? Kasim suddenly remembered his father's pride and embarrassment when he handed Kasim over to Kasim's first teacher. "'You can have the flesh, but leave me the bones,' eh?" Kasim laughed as he repeated the cliché which justified anything in the name of education. But the man didn't respond, except to turn and look out the window again.

Down the mountain the distinct points of the street lamps began to flicker and shine through the exhaust-filled haze which hung over the road. "Is that Damascus already?" the guy asked, nodding down toward the sickly glow of the city.

Yeah, dick head. What do you think it is? Paris? But Kasim kept his reply to himself.

On the sloping shoulders of the road, the empty spaces were beginning to fill with people and bicycles and the first lumbering city bus Kasim had spotted the whole trip. His fare too was watching the crowds. He turned his head to follow two boys who were miming a kick at the melon they'd just bought from a pile on the roadside.

"Pull over, Mister," the guy shouted with such urgency that Kasim made an emergency stop. He heard the driver behind scream at him, "Watch out, you son of a whore."

"Just wait here a minute," the man said and leapt out of the taxi. "What the hell . . ." Kasim muttered, then remembered the meter was still running.

The man brought back a couple of bags of fruit, and as Kasim accelerated away, he offered Kasim an apricot before taking one himself. "*Azeem*, wonderful," he sighed and took another apricot, then passed the bag forward to Kasim.

His hunger made something click. "You've been inside, haven't you?" Kasim mumbled through the soft, sweet pulp of the apricot. "In Sednayya, yeah?"

"Yes."

"A political?"

"Yes."

"How long?" Kasim asked, then wondered if the apricots had given him diarrhea of the mouth. He didn't want to know any of this stuff. It was better not to know.

"Eight years."

"Those not your clothes then?"

"No."

The guy had just got out. A writer, eh? Kasim found it difficult to keep his eyes on the road. He took another apricot and felt good about eating the same fruit as this fellow. Not that he had anything to do with politicals, he was too smart for that. But this was a bit special, a political eating apricots right in the back of his taxi. Kasim watched him carefully as the headlights of the other cars played over different parts of his face.

During the rest of the journey the two men sat in silence, the bag of apricots passing back and forth between them. When they finally got to El Jisr el Abiad, the man directed Kasim toward a back street which ended in a short flight of stairs. Kasim grunted with recognition and said, "Near the Qwaitly house, eh? What's it like to grow up in a President's shadow?" he said sarcastically, then regretted it. The man said nothing, only asked Kasim to stop the car in front of the apartment building on the left.

"The guard who helped find me the clothes also gave me a loan," the man said as he paid the fare. "Can you help me get up the stairs?"

To his surprise, Kasim found himself easing his bulk from under the steering wheel. He watched as the man stood stock-still looking up at the few scraggly plants which trailed through the railing around the lowest balcony and at the lengths of awning woven into the railings of those higher up. The flats seemed abandoned, their windows were so well-screened from view.

The man stumbled toward the entrance and grudgingly Kasim called after him, "Do you want me to come up too?"

The man grunted, pushed the time switch for the stairwell light and, with Kasim's help, began to climb, turning his head to read some of the graffiti as he went. Finally, when he came to a gray paneled door on the third landing, he stopped, sagged, then straightened, and pressed the bell, once, then once again more forcefully. Kasim waited against the yellowed wall a few steps below the landing.

A woman's voice called out through the door, "Who's there? Who are you?"

"It's Saddullah, Mother. Saddullah."

"What? Who are you?" the voice shrilled, and again the man called out, louder this time, "Saddullah, Mother. I'm home."

The doorway soon filled with others, a stooped, white-haired man, two young lads, and a smaller child still in her school uniform. The little girl pushed forward first and grabbed at the man's arm and danced up and down. Then the others came forward and clung to his neck, and his back, and pulled him into the apartment. Kasim too found himself sucked inside. The man's mother continued to hold onto his hand, as his father and brothers and little sister, one after the other, embraced Saddullah and broke their silence, first with laughter and then with homecoming tears.

Pressed against the coat rack in the vestibule, Kasim watched, unnoticed until he raised his hand to brush the wet from his face. Then, Saddullah's father, seeing Kasim, linking him with the blessing, took his hand and shook it again and again, "*Yatik el afiya*, Sir. Thank you, thank you." Kasim nodded, then slipped out the door and down the stairs.

In the car Kasim wiped his face on his sleeve and looked up quickly at the dark balcony before driving into the swirl of traffic at El Jisr el Abiad. At the traffic lights, he glanced in his mirror, half expecting to see the man. But he was gone. Only the portraits remained, looking backward, away from where Kasim's political had sat. When the red light turned, Kasim stepped on the gas and muttered "*Yatik el afiya*," thank you, to the lights.

NOT ONE OF US

"You're just like nigger-haters who've woken up to find themselves living in Harlem," Manal roared at Suad. It was an ugly thing to say to her older sister, but she was shaken by Suad's air of superiority. Manal was also shocked by how much she'd forgotten about being home.

"Well, maybe we are because that's the way it feels. Or maybe that's the way you make me feel. How could you dream of inviting that woman to my *istiqbaal*, to my afternoon party?"

The whine in Suad's reply pierced Manal's small reserve of patience.

"She gave a talk at one of the American Women's afternoon tea parties and it was good. At the Ambassador's residence," Manal said, forcing herself to be reasonable and matter-of-fact.

But Suad snapped back, "Someone said it was good. Well, so what? That woman has been in the air everywhere for over a year. Just because you arrive and hear about her for the first time, you think you've found a jewel. I don't care if that woman is welcome all over Damascus, she is not welcome in my house."

"Our house."

"My house in this case." Suad flushed and a rage of color spread quickly down her neck. "You're behaving just like one of those Americans, all interfering and gone tomorrow. And I don't think you understand any more about Damascus than they do."

"Oh, I understand a lot about Damascus. That's why I got out when I did." Manal wondered how she could ever have looked forward to coming back. She dragged her toe along one of the squares on the Turkmen carpet in the entrance hall, resenting the geometry of the design. Then she looked up and caught a glimpse of herself in the mirror. She was as young at fifty as Suad was old at fifty-five, as if the difference could be measured in decades rather than the five summers when Suad had been the only child.

"You got out, did you? All by yourself? It was me who encouraged you to go, and Daddy's money which paid for your fine degrees."

Manal looked at her turkey-gobbler sister, could see her chins and bosom quivering. Suad still treated her as if she were in graduate school and in need of long-distance care, even though Manal had a good job and a good life in the States.

"Suad, listen. The woman has done something brave. She's a Syrian who has dared to write about the country, about Damascus and Arab women. Wouldn't it be good to have a chance to meet her in person?"

"Maybe. But not in my house."

"Our house," Manal said again softly, before admitting, "I've already asked Fedwa to speak to her, to find out if she would consider coming to talk to us as well."

"You've already asked her?" Suad's voice cut through the air. "Without consulting me? How could you do that, Manal?"

"I haven't asked her yet, only asked Fedwa to find out if she'd come," Manal stumbled. "Of course I'd ask you first. That's what I'm doing now. And no, I haven't forgotten how you supported my education. But what is the point of it, if we don't try and learn something new."

"There is nothing new in this. *Kaatiba*, *mualiffa*, what nonsense! The woman isn't a writer, but an opportunist who's played on her connections. Think of her background. She's just not one of us. I don't want her here and that's all there is to it."

"Have you read the book?"

"No, and I don't need to. I've heard enough about it to last me a lifetime. That woman has a chip on her shoulder. The book makes a mockery of us. She can't reach the grapes, so she says they're sour." Suad's indignation made her forget the intellectual airs she was careful to give herself when Manal was around.

"Does it really make fun of us?"

"Of course it does. What about the lesbian scene at the hairdresser's? Do you think that's typical of life in Damascus? Anyway, you haven't read it either, so how dare you tell me what I should think?"

"I have finished it now. You do know that the woman has a doctorate in English literature, don't you? So of course I want to meet her," Manal said, reclaiming the one advantage she had in arguments with Suad.

Suad was so proper, and so critical. Manal noticed too that Suad's fury had made her swell up and dwarf the generous blue armchair in which she was sitting. She looked just like one of the fierce old ladies who'd terrorized them when they were kids. Hadn't they sworn they'd never grow up like that? Then when Suad began to twist and fiddle with her wedding ring, Manal knew she had forgotten. Manal silently cursed her long dead brother-in-law, suspecting that Suad used the ring to commune with her husband, to buttress her opinions with his certainty. Next she'll be talking about family responsibility and our good family name, Manal thought, and dug her toe into another square of the carpet.

"Suad," she said. "Suad, you really shock me. Why does this matter so much?"

"It matters because I'll lose every friend I have," Suad gulped. "You've always lived away; you don't understand." Her voice was edged with fear. The sound made Manal ache for her sister. At the same time it drew from deep inside her other things she'd forgotten about Damascus.

"But Suad," Manal defied the fear, "what kind of friends are they, if they are going to find the idea so terrible? I'm your sister and I don't think it's terrible."

"Maybe not, but you don't have to live here all the time," Suad said. Then she picked up her handbag and house keys and shooed Manal out the door as if Manal were a small child.

The sisters sat in silence, an uncomfortable silence, as the taxi took them to Mezze. Back in the privacy of the sidewalk Suad hissed, "Believe me, they won't want that woman to join us, so let's forget this whole business right now." Manal pursed her lips, but her reply was stifled by the sharp pink of the oleanders in front of Farah's flat. Was this the color of an *istiqbaal*, she thought, as memories of enforced proprieties came flooding back. "Okay," she said meekly, "but I do owe the woman the courtesy of asking."

Farah opened the door herself. She was winter white and courtly in a deep blue suit and jewelry obviously chosen to be discreet. *"Ahlan wa Sahlan,"* Welcome, How delightful to see you. *"Ahlan wa Sahlan."* Her greetings were sticky and so effusive they made Manal nauseous. Perhaps she had become a stranger here after all.

Farah was Suad's oldest friend. They'd been at the French school together and even married in the same year. Just after the baccalaureate, and both to men who'd trained as lawyers. They have a lot in common, Manal thought. It was meant as a neutral observation, but other memories began to sting, reminding her how they'd always enjoyed patronizing her and how she would always be Suad's clever little sister who had never married, poor thing, and had to make do with a career instead of a husband and family.

"Come in, please," Farah said. "We're all here and were just waiting for you to arrive." Manal caught Suad's sideways glance which said very clearly that it was all her fault that they were late. Suad's injunction to silence was still hissing in Manal's head and the self-doubt had begun. She'd forgotten a lot; perhaps Suad was right about the need to be circumspect.

"Manal, it's wonderful to have you with us again," Farah continued seamlessly, "You'll be staying for some months this time. A sabbatical, Suad said, and well deserved, I'm sure."

"Yes, I'm home for six months. It's wonderful to be back," Manal replied, hearing herself mimic the cloying lilt of Farah's voice.

Bobbing her head with good-natured ease, Suad greeted the room full of women, then settled herself at one end of a deep sofa where her round figure was balanced by the bulk of the smiling woman at the other. Meanwhile Farah took Manal by the arm and towed her round the room making sure that she knew and remembered each of the women who belonged to their visiting circle.

Nodding greetings in Farah's wake, it amused Manal to think that, because of their row, Suad had let her come out without scolding her for wearing dark trousers and a long jacket rather than a tight, waisted suit, or one of the fussy dresses, which were the unofficial uniform of the group. But as she listened to Farah reminding the women that she was now a Professor of Comparative Literature at SUNY, she realized that Farah was doing Suad's scolding for her. "The State University of New York in Albany,"

Farah said, emphasizing each word with an unwarranted precision. There was a polite lack of interest in the women's murmured responses.

Manal had forgotten how effortlessly sweet her own greetings should have been and she almost sighed out loud when Farah finally showed her to the one remaining chair tucked into a corner. From her outpost she looked round at the fourteen or fifteen women in the circle and, as she did so, the phrase "dowdy dowagers" popped into her head. She smiled at the English alliteration and toyed with a possible translation, but nothing in Arabic seemed as telling.

The salon was large and light and the conservatory which extended along its length opened out into a garden hedged with oleanders flowering beneath the high wall. A suitable habitat, Manal thought, as the women turned to their neighbors and began to gabble like ungainly, flightless birds. She tried to listen, but the gossip was too local and inbred; she couldn't get any purchase on what was being said. She didn't know whose daughter had committed suicide, and clearly couldn't ask, though she did sit forward and nod alertly in the hope that someone would tell her—but they didn't. Nor did they bother to ask if she had any advice for the nephew who wanted to sell his clinic in Aleppo and work as a dentist in Abu Dhabi. And of course she had no advice to give. And other things just didn't make sense: Were they really talking about elephants at the Sheraton, or had Damascus simply become a zoo? Manal glanced round at the well-groomed women. If it were a zoo, then surely they thought of themselves as spectators, not unfamiliar creatures on display.

She retreated from the conversation and was admiring the way the sunlight filtered into the room and added a hint of ochre to the pale walls when, a few seats away, a raddled woman with frosted hair began to knead a fine embroidered handkerchief into a tight ball. The woman was fighting tears which threatened to wash her heavy makeup into the ravines of her wrinkles. She explained to the circle of attentive faces how proud they'd been to send the daughter to college in the States, how clever the daughter was, and beautiful, of course; yet now, four years later—the woman paused and her breath caught—the daughter had put on the veil and turned to Islam to reclaim women's rights. As Manal listened to the mother's incomprehension and the clucks of disapproval from the others, she decided she had more than a sneaking sympathy for the daughter's Islamist cause. Manal stopped listening to the clichés of commiseration when she noticed, behind the woman's bowed head, a splendidly muted oil painting. But her appreciation of Farah's good taste lasted only a moment, until she realized that either the oil had been chosen to match the other colors in the room, or the room, and all the women in it, had been decorated to tone in with the painting. Whichever way, Manal felt cheated, and out of place.

She caught a glimpse of a small plain woman, Farah's maid, moving silently between the kitchen and the dining room. The maid was carrying plates of fruit and cake to the dining table where a silvered samovar, flanked by a blue Wedgwood teapot on one side and a jar of Nescafé on the other, was already steaming behind a careful display of porcelain cups and saucers. This was the sign Manal had been waiting for and, indeed, it was only a matter of minutes before Farah stood and addressed her guests. "My dears, I know it's Ramadan and that some of you are fasting, but I felt it would be discourteous to the rest of you not to offer something to eat. So please, come and help yourselves."

The women stirred and two of the Christian ladies and a woman who was someone's cousin visiting from the Lebanon, collected platefuls of cakes and tea. Suad and Manal were also Christians but, as Suad had made clear while they'd waited for the taxi, her rule—never to eat in front of others who are fasting—was one which Manal would also do well to observe.

When they were all seated again, Farah turned to Suad. "I'm right in thinking, am I not, that it's your turn

to have us next month?" Suad nodded contentedly and
Manal realized that she had absolutely no intention of
mentioning the invitation. So be it, Manal thought; well, I
shall. But it did cross her mind that it might be easier if
she were wearing the militant daughter's protective veil.

"Suad and I are looking forward to welcoming you on
the fifteenth of next month. And, as you all know, I've
been abroad a lot, but now that I'm back, I thought it
might be fun to do something special."

The women murmured to their neighbors and then
looked back at Manal expectantly.

"Well," Manal said. She paused for effect, pleased
that she wasn't a teacher for nothing, "Well, I've been intrigued by the new book on women in Damascus and I'd
like to invite the author to join us."

The silence followed Manal's intervention was broken only by one of the ladies gulping down a mouthful of
scalding tea. Manal could see Suad drawing herself up
with such ire that she feared that her sister was going to
cry out, "'*Ayb*! For shame; '*ayb*!" and scold Manal as she'd
done when they were little. But before Suad could speak,
Farah smiled and said smoothly, "Oh, that would be a
novelty. But you know, we've all become so used to doing
things the way we do them, we're probably too old for
change." And from elsewhere in the room, comfortable,
self-deprecating laughter echoed Farah's own.

"But," Manal continued, "I'm sure you would enjoy
meeting her."

Farah began another genteel feint, but she was interrupted by Suad's companion on the sofa. The woman
reached out and patted Suad's hand, then turned and
asked sharply, "Manal, have you already invited her?"

"Oh, no. Of course not," Suad hastened to assure her
friend with a tight smile. Then Suad got up from her end
of the sofa and walked slowly toward the dining room.

"No, we haven't invited her yet," Manal replied,
while watching her cowardly sister take one of the delicate cups, add a couple of spoons of Nescafé and draw
water from the samovar. "I wanted to ask you first. Not

because I thought you'd mind, of course, but because it would make the *istiqbaal* rather more formal if she came to talk to us about the book."

"Oh well, if it was only an idea, then there's no problem," the woman on the sofa said, comforting Suad with a smile.

The raddled woman with the born-again daughter intervened: "Well, I certainly don't think it's a good idea." Her voice was so strident that Manal's sympathy for the daughter doubled. It doubled again as the other women in the room added their agreement.

After this, there was a self-congratulatory silence and Manal could see by the way the women relaxed back into their chairs that they thought the matter was settled. She started to speak again, but was interrupted almost before she'd begun.

Selwa, who unlike the others made no attempt to squeeze the last drops of glamour from her middle-aged body, spoke with severity, "No, we don't want to meet her. After all, our meetings are to do with friendship, not politics."

"Politics, Selwa?" Manal asked, knowing without a shadow of doubt that Selwa was talking about something far more important than formal power. "Politics?" she asked again. She was beginning not to care.

"Yes, politics," Selwa replied. "You do know, of course, she's an Ala . . ."

Anticipating Selwa's indiscretion, Farah swooped gracefully into the conversation before Selwa could finish the dangerous word. "At the reading circle I asked why I should want to read *The Bonfire of the Vanities* or want to know about that class of people in the Bronx? Manal," she urged gently. "I think the same question is appropriate now. Why didn't she write about a better class of people, or show how people can improve themselves?"

"But that's exactly what she is writing about; how she'd grown up in a village . . . ," Manal started, but Farah, widening her eyes and tilting her head slightly to one side, forced Manal to stop.

"And that's exactly what I mean," Selwa was determined to have her say. "The woman grows up in a village, but then she writes about the killing of a village
girl. It's sensationalism. She should know very well that
even among her own people such an incident may happen only once in a lifetime. And, it certainly has nothing
to do with us. So why did she chose to expose us to
ridicule by writing in English about such things?"

"Wouldn't you both like to ask her and perhaps find
out?" Manal asked, looking first at Farah and then
Selwa. There was an edge in her voice.

"Absolutely not," Farah said; she was clearly angry
that Manal had dared to re-enter the conversation.
Farah's disdain was fearsome and Manal could see Suad,
in the dining room, standing perfectly still like a rabbit
hoping to escape the jackal's gaze. Farah's "absolutely
not" also stilled the others, but their voices soon rose
again from all sides of the room. Manal, Pandora, My
God, what have I started? Manal was amazed at the
rush to protect Damascene privilege. At least this isn't
boring, she thought grimly and pursed her lips with a
stubbornness she remembered from childhood.

"You do know," a woman whose dress matched the
oleanders in the garden took over the interrogation.
"You do know that when that woman spoke to the Americans, she was saying all kinds of things—about the
Women's Union working for nursery education but not
for women's rights; about women in parliament and lack
of change. Now, that may sound all right to you, Manal,"
she said archly, "but quite simply, I just wouldn't feel
able to come. I'm sorry, Suad," she said, nodding toward
the dining room, "but I have to think of my husband's
position."

Manal stared at this shocking-pink woman and remembered now how color alone could impose good behavior. And she tried to imagine why attending Suad's
istiqbaal would be more political, and more compromising, than being the wife of a government minister. It
wasn't even as if the book had been censored.

Selwa interrupted again. Manal could see the others flinch, anticipating another indiscretion. "I heard she was introduced, by the American Ambassador's wife, as the Syrian Benazir Bhutto. That tells you how little the Americans understand. Can you imagine saying that about someone who is so close to the government? Everybody knows that she worked for the security services when she was abroad."

Farah's hands began to press down on her thighs. To make sense of what was happening, Manal forced herself to unravel some of the issues and, in doing so, she found she had a lot of sympathy for the Americans' confusion. First, she thought, it is the Alawite, and not the minister's wife, who is close to the government and, secondly, no one, Alawite or not, wants to be seen as a political challenge. Manal felt a prickling horror. She had forgotten the first rule of Damascene etiquette, that such topics were never broached in public, however sure the gathering.

Farah too was aware of the risks and, to distract Selwa from further indiscretions, and to lead them all back to safer ground, she said, "Manal, we're not interested in what that woman has to say about Arab feminism or those women who first removed their veils. Nor are we very interested," she added, looking pointedly at the woman with the daughter, "in latter day feminists who've put the veil back on again." Manal followed Farah's glance and, behind the unfortunate woman, she saw Suad still pretending to sip her Nescafé.

"Actually that woman seems to blame everything on Islam," Selwa almost shouted. "And we can all guess why she's doing that. They lack the education to be good Muslims. We are different, Manal. She is simply not one of us."

There was a murmur of agreement, and the faces of the other women made it clear they thought Manal was either very stupid or very treacherous or both. They were relieved that Selwa had finally managed to speak out plainly.

Manal turned toward the dining room and would have liked to smile a "sorry" at her sister, but although Suad caught her glance, she gave no sign of recognition. Manal was beginning to get very angry.

"Ladies, ladies," she cried, "Surely, you're all taking this far too seriously. Really, I did think it might be interesting, but," she smiled gingerly, "I can see you don't share my opinion," and I hope, she thought fiercely, I don't reek of your Chanel and self-satisfaction.

No one responded to Manal's attempt at appeasement until the Lebanese woman, heedless of those who were fasting, lit up a cigarette, then said, "Well, I'd be interested in hearing what she has to say for herself." Manal nodded, rather wishing she also dared to ask the woman for a cigarette, when the woman added, "But if she did come, I don't think we'd want to have any discussion afterward." Manal could find no reply to this smug compromise and simply stared at the elegant woman with disbelief.

Then the minister's wife stood up and tugged at her gaudy pink dress, "Farah, thank you so much for today, but I must be going. And," she paused and turned toward Suad who was still standing by the samovar, "you must of course do what you think is right, but, as I said, I won't feel able to come if that woman is going to be there too."

Farah took the woman's arm and walked with her to the door. She looked back toward the salon and said in an unusually loud voice, "Don't worry, I'm sure we'll sort something out in time for Suad's turn."

What had to be done was done even before Farah returned. The women retreated from the invitation as if from the plague, but, Manal now knew, they would associate poor Suad with the contagion for a very long time to come.

In the taxi on the way home Suad pressed herself as close as possible to the far door. Tamed by the necessary silence, they were tense, each waiting for the perfect moment to pounce on the other. When the taxi left the empty tree-lined streets near Farah's, Manal watched as more and more people appeared on the pavements until they were jostling each other and spilling into the road so close to the cars that they could have reached out and touched the taxi had they wanted to. Then, up the hill on the other side of the river, the people began to disappear until only the bougainvillea was left to spill color out toward the road. During the journey, neither Manal nor Suad spoke, nor did their eyes meet, even once.

With the keys shaking in her hand, Suad opened the door and when she got inside she dropped her handbag, sank into the blue chair which now dwarfed her trembling body, and crumpled in tears. "Manal, how could you have done that to me? I told you what would happen. I told you what they'd think."

Manal reached down to comfort her sister. "Yes, you did tell me and I'm sorry. Sorry for you," she said. "But not for me. My god, Suad, they are so bigoted. It is *tazyeeff*, unreal, their sense of entitlement. What's happened to you, Suad?"

"Nothing's happened to me," Suad sobbed, "nothing, until today, that is."

"For god's sake, Suad, nothing much has happened today either. The prosperous few have always been outnumbered, but it's as if this lot have only just noticed that some of the others have demanded a share of the spoils. What do they want, a ghetto walled with gold?"

"I don't know. But a lot has happened today. It's much more complicated than you think. That woman is dangerous, Manal. She's not to be trusted. You know, when things go wrong, people attach themselves to their own kind."

"Yes, I understand that. But how do you identify 'one's own kind'?" Manal asked, and, in that moment, she resolved to meet the woman somewhere for a coffee.

THE BOX (1959)

"Teta, what's that?" the little girl's question was muffled. She was lying on her tummy, white socks waggling in the air as her finger traced a complicated journey along the arabesques of the carpet. "Grandmother, what's that?" Hind asked again, this time raising her head to address the great wide back of her granny who was watering the jade plant on the balcony.

"What did you say?" the old woman replied, relieved to straighten her knees as she turned toward the doorway. The child pointed under the narrow bed. "That," she said. "That box. What's in it?"

Knowing the child would persist until she had an answer, the old woman put down the watering can and moved slowly across the small room to peer under the bed. She sighed and said gently, "It's my funeral box, Habeebeti."

Hind sat up and tucked her feet carefully under the gathers of her dress. "What does that mean, Teta?" she asked in a subdued voice.

"A funeral box . . ." The old woman paused. She sank down slowly onto the chair facing the child, "When I was a girl, Hind, every bride had a funeral box. In it are the things that will be needed when I die."

"What things, Teta?" Hind asked softly.

The old woman looked at the child, at her serious face. "You're too little to be so curious," she scolded, then sighed again. "There's a winding sheet in the box, a winding sheet brought back by my father from Mecca. And rose oil, and camphor and cloths to wash my body. But I'm not dead yet," she smiled, her blue eyes lighting the folds of her face. The child's face widened, then sparkled at the joke.

"But, Teta, why did you need a box?"

"Only God knows when we'll die, Habeebeti. And in those days when a bride left her family she had to be very grown up."

But I didn't feel grown up. My stomach ached when his sister came to our house, when she watched me serve her coffee. But my hands didn't tremble. I kept them from trembling, kept my eyes down, like the nuns who flowed down the corridors with the scent of lilies. And she couldn't have seen the trembling inside me. Couldn't have seen my thoughts, my dreams of marrying my cousin Wa'el. I hated her when she accepted me, accepted a second cup of sweet coffee. He saw her coming from school, she said, he saw her and fell in love, and he wants her for his bride.

"Did cousin Ruwayda have a box when she got married?" Hind asked.

Her grandmother raised her chin and made a quiet click with her tongue. "No, it's not the same. Now it's easier to be a bride," and she saw little Hind in her starched pink dress dancing in the circle around Ruwayda, the bride. "It's easier now."

Hind nodded gravely, then giggled, "Teta, I ate two pieces of cake at Ruwayda's wedding."

"You'll get fat like me and then who will you marry?"

Hind twisted her shoulders and tossed her head in a flirt, "I'll marry whoever I want," Hind said and stretched to hold hands with herself behind her back.

> *I didn't want him before our engagement, before the* aqd en-nikah *was agreed and the* moulid *prayers for the Prophet's birth were sung. He's far too old, and he has another wife, my mother said. But he talked to Father, met him day after day. We're Circassians, he's an Arab, it will be very difficult, my mother said. He's an educated man, Father replied, he'll be proud of an educated wife. She is only fifteen and he is nearly forty, my sister argued. He has daughters her age by the first wife who will hate his fair new bride. I'll be able to protect her, my Grandfather said, and he was the chief of police. The French used us, the Circassians, as their watchdogs over the Arabs. She could be a teacher, let her continue her studies, my sister said. They are aghas, they own vast acres of land, it's hard for Father to refuse, mother said. The mahr he will pay is high, they all said together, and he will give her a beautiful house in Beirut as part of the marriage settlement.*

Hind was still swaying, delighting herself with her knowing answer when her grandmother looked down again. "Impertinent little coquette," the old woman said.

"So Habeebeti, tell me, will you marry this husband of yours for love?"

"Of course," Hind replied, indignantly. The old woman smiled at the child's certainty.

> *Yes, marry for love, little one. I didn't at first, but I did in the end. My parents were modern, and my father was a liberal man. And after the* kitab, *they welcomed my fiance to our house and he came often to visit me. We sat high in the house on the long, low window seats in the men's salon, my grandfather's room, which was warmed by a stove lit early.*
>
> *My auntie worked her bright embroidery silks in the corner by the fire, but the pictures we made were our own.*
>
> *As we looked down at the river, the winter sunlight would touch his face and he'd speak of Paris, where he'd finished his education and become a young man about town. He took me to meet friends in cafés along Boulevard St. Germain, and we spied on Tuilerie lovers and flew to Chantilly from the Tour d'Eiffel. While I listened, timid Aysha, our maid, would bring us coffee with cardamoms and bowls of walnuts and apples. And when she'd slip back to the kitchen, she'd steal a pinch of our love and use it to scent her dreams.*
>
> *After coffee, we'd change places, my fiancé and I, and he'd draw out my stories with expectation in his eyes. I'd tell him tales of our family and those of the nuns at my stiff convent school. Or as he leaned deep into the cushions, I would read from a favorite novel, or sometimes the verse of Verlaine. . . . Je fais souvent ce rêve étrange et pénétrant . . . Thus, we talked and laughed, and I fell in love. Have you fallen in love? he'd ask, with your Sheikh of Araby? he'd tease, and I'd say yes, oh yes, and then pretend to swoon.*

"Teta," Hind reached up and patted her grand-mother's knee. "Have you gone to sleep, Teta?"

"What? What's that, Habeebeti?" The old woman shook herself, stirred by the child's concern. "No, not asleep, Hind. Just remembering. When you are as old as I am, you'll also have many memories which keep you busy." Then she paused, reached out and stroked the child's head before asking, "So what will be in your trousseau, my little Hind?"

"I don't know, Teta; I don't want a box."

"No, not a box, but you'll want lots of lovely dresses, and earrings, and other pretty things."

"Did you have pretty things, Teta?"

"Circassian brides were famous for their trousseaux," the old woman said, sitting back in the chair. "For the wedding I had ten dresses, all made to Paris patterns, ten silk dresses in every color of a pea-cock's tail. And gold earrings with tiny diamonds, and gold bracelets and a necklace of pearls. Yes, I had many, many pretty things."

My father bought back his pride with my trousseau. He went from Homs to Damascus and returned with a treasure of cloth and jewels worth more than the mahr *itself. And when the bridal trunks were loaded on carriages to be taken to my husband's house, men and boys crowded the street to catch the tiny glittering coins which were thrown to bless our marriage and to protect us from the evil eye. In the* agha's *great palace, my trousseau was spread out for his family to see: the glass lamps and cooking pots, the china plates and all my embroidery—the ice crystals on soft white napkins, the flowered towels and gardens of scarves and all twenty sheets with their intricate borders. I knew that his mother and sisters and his brother's wives—no, I didn't think then of his other wife—would be amazed and would say to each other, look at her skill and delicate taste.*

*Then they'd add, shining with pleasure, our bride
went to the French school; she's an educated girl
as well.*

"Will I have more earrings than these, Teta?" Hind
asked, spinning the tiny hoops with her hands.

"Oh yes, many pairs of earrings, Habeebeti. Those
are very plain, they are just the beginning, but I wanted
you to have them, they are the only ones I have left."

"What happened to the rest of your earrings, Teta?"

"They were sold, Hind, a long time ago. But there
are so many other things to tell you about the old days.

*The bride's bath came first. We'd mocked the
custom, my school friends and I, but on the day
they came to the house, I was happy when they
giggled and gave me presents of soap and a looking glass, and beautiful handkerchiefs and a fine
ivory comb. Then, like the parcels of cake and
bowls of yellow quinces, they bundled me up, and
held both my hands as we walked to the women's
hammam. In the house of fire, on the* chaudière's
*marble bench, the old women scrubbed me with
bath cloths until my skin tingled red and I
thought my hair—it was light brown and long—
would be tugged out by the roots. They used old-
fashioned* beyloon haleby, *my mother and aunties,
to scent my hair with sandalwood as they sang
songs of the perfumed bride. And how my friend,
Nazira, blushed when they said she'd be next.*

"Did you wear a white dress, like Ruwayda, when
you got married, Teta?"

"A white dress . . . ? Yes, I wore a white dress."

*A white dress à la Franka and strapped shoes
and a band of roses in my hair when I left my father's house. When I sat between his fat sister, and
mine, in his car, draped inside and out in pink*

*muslin with bouquets of roses on the doors. I was
proud of my dress that evening, at the party where
so many women, his sisters and cousins, swirled
dancing in lush Turkish velvets while I sat still
and demure on the bride's throne.*

*It was dazzling at first, then oppressive, as
the air became heavy with noise. I felt faint when
the old women approached me or laughed at the
singer's coarse jokes. Then, at the end of the party
when the heat of the gathering was intense, he
came, holding the arm of an old man, the only two
men in the room. I stood and honored his father
by bowing and kissing his hand. Then my husband, as tall as a pine tree, gathered me up from
my throne and we swayed like the wind as we
danced to the center of the room. He whispered:
They say, if the bride dances, her luck dances too.
Then he magicked me back to the present and I
laughed boldly, too boldly perhaps, when he
added, how lovely you look, my wife à la Franka,
when you dance to harmonium, tambourine, and
drums.*

*Then he led me across the courtyard, away
from the women of the house. The moon was setting behind us when we stopped in the silence and
cool and looked toward the morning sky. He settled me down in our chamber, on the great covered bed, and he offered me water and sweetmeats
and slipped off my shoes with his hands. You
must be exhausted, my love, you've been up getting ready since morning. Lie down and sleep, my
sweet little Franka, we'll do things à la Parisi-
enne today.*

The child had begun to trace new journeys along the
carved wooden patterns on the arm of the chair and the
old woman, grateful for her patience, nodded, "Yes, I
wore a white dress, Habeebeti." Then she got up and
slowly crossed the room.

Bending stiffly to take a small packet tied with blue
ribbon from the drawer at the bottom of her wardrobe,
she glanced back at her granddaughter's expectant face
and said, "Hind, come here and see. This is our wedding
photograph. It was taken in Beirut during our *voyage de
noces*. In 1926. More than thirty years ago. Can you imagine that, my six-year-old Hind? It was a long time ago."

"Oh, Teta, you were very beautiful."

*Yes, they said I was a beauty. He was very
handsome. When the photographer saw how tall
he was, and how the top of my head barely
reached his handkerchief pocket, the photographer
smiled and arranged us so that he sat on the chair
with me standing beside him with my hand on his
shoulder. I was proud to stand next to him like
that.*

"But your dress was short, Teta. Cousin Ruwayda's
was long and swung out from her in a big circle," Hind
said, spinning around until she began to wobble and collapsed giggling.

"Yes, it was short and very fashionable then. And do
you see," she pointed, "your grandfather even wore spats,
he was also a fashionable man."

"Why did he wear them, Teta? Did he have feet like
a duck," Hind's eyes had widened, then she laughed with
glee at the silly idea.

"Now, Hind. Do you think he looks like a duck?" And
the child dimpled, then shook her head gravely.

"Teta, I can make duck noises . . ."

*He made such gentle sounds as he rustled the
skirt of my dress to make a place next to me on the
bed. Wake up, my sweet Franka, or you'll sleep
your wedding night through. Then he kissed my
cheek, then my ear. Soft, nuzzling, lingering kisses
as I lay half-asleep, feeling the warmth which
moved down me till it reached the tips of my toes.*

He was calm and strong as he lifted me up and cupped my face in his hands and waited for me to wake.

When I smiled, he laughed quietly and I could feel his breath on my face. Then his eyes flew over my dress and he said, Here, let's get this off you, my beautiful Frankish bride. He teased and became a mock-tiger, growling and biting my arms, worrying the buttons which fastened the sleeve dragging at my wrist. Then taking my other hand, he growled fiercely once again. Look, he said, Look, these loops have learned better, and his hands were as sure as my mother's as he freed my left sleeve and my ring. Then he grimaced and pretended despair, as he spied the sets of back buttons which held me tight in the dress. Velvet lips like a pony he nibbled until one set was undone, then he groaned and said, I'm impatient, I'll tiger the next set away.

The dress slipped down off of my shoulders, I felt his hands touch my back. Then he let his long fingers stroke me, saying, Sweet, you are shivering, from cold?, and he reached a long arm for my nightdress folded carefully at the foot of the bed. I looked at his eyes and dark eyebrows as he floated the dress over my head. The nightdress rested ruched around my waist as he reached to touch my silk stockings before gently unveiling my legs.

"Teta, look at me, I'm a duck. Teta, you're falling asleep again."

"No, darling, I'm not asleep. I was thinking of Beirut and our three years there before your mother was born. See, Habeebeti," she said, shuffling through the small collection of photographs which nestled on her lap as if they had never been put away. "Look, here is your grandfather. We'd gone high up the mountain to Shimlan for a picnic. Do you see the baskets, and the man—that was

his friend Omar—making a cooking fire under the pines?
That day the cicadas were noisy above us as we drank
jugfuls of lemonade. Then, after the sun had set and the
wind had changed, we found a carriage and went clatter-
ing back down to Beirut."

The little girl stood and leaned against her grandmother's knee, peering down at the brown photograph.
"Is that you, Teta? With flowers on your dress and your
hair all short and curly." The child paused, then looked
fondly at her grandmother, "You look very happy, Teta."

"Yes, for those three years I was very happy, Habeebeti. Your grandfather's business flourished and we had
many friends. We spun in a whirl of picnics, and tea
dances and evening parties. We even had a piano in
Beirut and your grandfather would ask me to play for our
guests. He was proud of me, Hind. He was a good man."

"I didn't know you could play the piano, Teta. I want
to learn too. Maman says if I'm good, I can start to take
proper lessons next year."

"That's good, Habeebeti, but you'll have to practice
very hard. Why don't you sing me a song you'd like to
play on the piano. I like hearing you sing."

*For three years there was music until his fa-
ther died and we had to leave Beirut. I was carrying our child and my belly was round and taut. I
was fearful of leaving our wise Doctor Suhail and
afraid that my child, who played skipping games
in my belly, would meet trouble as soon as it came.
But he teased the fear from my heart and prismed
it in the light, then juggled the fragments of color
into a rainbow dance.*

*He scared my fears to death with earthquak-
ing, volcanic bandits who were waiting, waiting,
he whispered and slid his eyes sideways in terror,
waiting in ambush round the next corner of the
mountain road. When he said this, I was sure the
baby had heard, because it kicked so hard my
dress fluttered up. Then with his eyes round on my*

belly, he said with dark portent, our situation must be truly dire if even our baby is trying to run away. And as I leaned into a belly-wobbling laugh, I watched a young boy climb out of scrub near the roadside, a skinny boy who divided his energy between carrying firewood and growing so fast that his old brown jellabiyyah *barely reached his knees. You see, he said grimly, that boy is a sentry, and he pointed eagle-high to where the great stone ramparts of Qalat el Hosn dominated the winding road.*

Stop worrying about my family, he said, they'll like you, because you're kind, and because I'm head of household now that my father has died. He sounded so sure that I couldn't then ask what his first wife would say, but picked up the globe of his courage and juggled it back in return. So rabb el beit, *my exalted household god, must I now fear you instead? He nodded then, like the doctor, Ah, I see you are feeling better, my dear. And I grinned at his cure in return. Then, more earnestly he added, My sharp little Franka, I fear boredom will be your worst enemy in my father's house. We won't stay there long, but while you are there, you must learn to be happy when the baby cries and gives you something to do, or grateful when a morning dove visits the courtyard for bread, or pleased when a bluebottle stirs up a breeze with its wings.*

When Hind finished singing snatches of a lover's lament by Feruz, the old woman smiled. "That was lovely, Habeebeti, but surely there are lighter verses for you to sing?"

"But I like those songs, Teta. Mother sings them all the time."

"Then sing me another one, but Habeebeti, always remember, Feruz's songs can make sadness sweet, but real grief is bitter, so bitter it curls your tongue and seeps from your liver like gall."

"Why do you say that, Teta?" Hind paused, then asked, "Did you always live in Beirut, before you came to live with us?"

"No, we had to leave Beirut, just before your mother was born. For a year we lived in the great house of your great-grandfather, your grandfather's father. But sing another song for me. I like to listen, little one."

When we reached the plain the air was dust-dry and hot as the mouth of an oven. My skin prickled with salt and I could see a drenching of sweat down his back. I was so hot I feared I would melt and leave the babe unborn and exposed to the sun on the seat of the car. As we neared his father's house, we saw how the heat had baked the land and left the people like burnt raisins, discarded at the edge of the road. There were beggars huddled in front of the mosque—thin, dirty children and women who sat with their backs to the wall and their legs out-stretched under pieces of ragged cloth. And when we turned into the courtyard, a dust devil twisted out to greet us and stung our faces with grit.

The baby came that night, our first night in his father's house, before the earth of the old man's grave had settled. When the pains began, he called his mother and roused his brothers' wives— though my cowife he left to sleep. And by midnight these strange agha women filled the room and sur-rounded me on our bed. I writhed in terror, but my baby was bolder than I and she slipped easily into her father's house. My little daughter, my Malika, was born into the dripping heat, and her grand-mother, his mother, whose hands were gnarled and her back bent double, took the babe and washed her gently with rosewater and scented my daughter's birth. Then the old woman brought me a sweet drink of cinnamon, as darkly red as my blood. Come child, drink, she said. It was a good birth and your daughter is healthy and fortunate.

*In these terrible times, it is men who carry the
burdens. She said it as a kindness, but I knew it
was a lie: he wanted, she wanted, and I had
prayed for a son to follow him, a son to become my
own tiny* agha, *and make me feel safe in his house.*

*That same night in the courtyard under a
hanging moon, my husband learned from his
brothers what had happened while we'd lived in
Beirut. There had been no rain during those three
years and the land was covered in red dust which
blew in with the desert storms. His father, more
muddled and mean than his brothers dared
admit, had refused their advice when the estate
harvests had brought in nothing. In the winter of
the third year, the villagers had become so hungry
that many had eaten their seed corn, and the stu-
pidly stubborn old tyrant began to sell things from
the house—a fine horse and carriage, then carpets
and the pearl inlay cupboards from the men's
salon. He'd sold them cheap, to a merchant from
Damascus, in return for more seed corn. Sold
them piece by piece, without asking his sons, until
there was nothing left to sell but the women's precious gold. And after that, when there was nothing
left to sell, except the great palace house and the
village lands, the old man died of shame.*

"Teta, that was a happy song. But you're still sad.
Why are you always sad, Teta?"

"We lived through terrible times just after your
mother was born. It didn't rain for three years and your
great-grandfather lost all his money and then died of a
broken heart." The child looked puzzled and began to ask
another question, when the old woman added, "It is hard
for me to know how to be happy, Hind, but I like it when
you are here."

*There was no time for loving during that ter-
rible year. He worked very hard to save us from*

*ruin. And night after night, when he came home
from the villages, I washed out his dusty* jellibiyah
*in a shallow pan to save water for his bath. And
when he could do nothing more, he came to me
and begged me to forgive him, begged me to help
him by selling my gold. And he took my diamond
earrings, and my necklace of pearls and then later
he begged me to forgive him and said we must sell
my house in Beirut.*

"Teta, I like being with you better than with Maman,
she never has time to tell me stories."

"Stories? Are they stories? Yes, Habeebeti, I too like
to talk to you, but some stories can be very sad."

"What happened when all the water went away,
Teta?"

"It was very hard for your grandfather that year
your mother was born and, at the end of that year, we
traveled once more to Beirut. I dressed your mother in
cloth from one of my peacock dresses. It nearly touched
the ground when she reached up to clasp hold of his finger. 'Baba,' she said, and that day she walked for the
very first time."

The old woman shuffled again through the photographs which had been resting on her knees and said,
"Habeebeti, come and see. This is a photograph of your
mother. Do you see what a lovely child she was? It was
taken in Beirut. It is the only photograph I have of the
three of us together."

"Where's grandfather now, Teta?"

"He's gone now, Hind. He died in Beirut."

"Did he die on a picnic, Teta?"

"No, he died just a year after your mother was born."

Hind looked down at the photograph again and
punched her finger at the chubby child, "Did she make it
bad for you, Teta?"

"No, Hind. Your mother was a good little girl, a good
child just like you."

But nothing else was good. He closed his publishing business and we bundled our house away. But he insisted we crate and box my piano. It will be our ark in the desert, he said.

It was hot when the men, the laboring men with their jellabiyyahs *tugged up round their waists, came to pack my piano. And he stood with them to ensure the work was well done. But he cared too much for my music, loved my music with his very life. Suddenly he cried out and fell down. Fell down, and I ran to him and he was whimpering in pain and then, in a moment, it was over and he was still and silent and dead.*

His brothers arrived the next day and ordered cars for us all. They made me sit with the coffin, with my babe in the peacock dress. They made me ride with the coffin as we drove up the twisting road. He was not there to tease me, to juggle my fears with his kindness, and I cried until somehow in weakness I knew what I had to do. I opened the door beside me and held my small child in my arms and, as I threw us onto the roadside, I hoped that we both would die.

"Teta, why are you so quiet? When people are very sad, can't they ever be happy again?" Hind said, and she leaned over the chair and stroked her grandmother's head. "Teta, it's time to wake up now. Mother has just called. Lunch will be ready soon."

The old woman shuddered, then said, "Habeebeti, don't worry, I'm fine. But I don't think I want any lunch today. You go on down to eat with your mother. I need to sit here and think for a bit."

When we returned to the great house, I knew they hated us then. Not his old mother, for in grief she had followed her son to the grave. But the rest, my cowife, his brothers, they were ready to claim

*what was left for themselves. I was the cherished
Circassian and my baby his heir by my body and
their jealousy knew no bounds. I was filled with
terrible dread, I cried every night for my child.
And one day, I watched my cowife stand impas-
sively as my sweet Malika stumbled close to the
well, and as I ran to save her, I felt my cowife's ha-
tred spit at me and I shivered when she laughed
at my fear. My cowife took over the cooking, and
could have poisoned our dishes with ease. Had I
not watched her like a tigress, she'd have had seen
us gone in a week. The day of my dresses was hor-
rible, it confirmed the doubts that I had. I'd
washed my silks out carefully and hung them out
on the line and when I returned to collect them, I
found them trampled in the byre. I screamed and
shook with terror, and huddled with my daughter,
weeping and cringing next to the cow's stall.*

*With that they had what they wanted, and
they called for my father to come. Your daughter is
mad, she can't stay here, they explained, and as I
wept out my story, he saw that I was very ill. He
wanted to take me home, and they said, yes of
course, but the little girl must stay here, for she is
her father's child. I screamed no, please leave me,
I cannot be parted from Malika. For two more
weeks we lived in the hell hole, sweet little Malika
and I. We stayed all that time in the chamber
where once I'd been a bride. I dared not move from
the place where his ghost could lie by my side, but
his sharp little Franka had vanished, and a mad
woman had become his wife.*

*Then my grandfather went to the judge in the
town and said, you may be in the pay of the aghas
but I want both my children home. And he
grabbed the judge's beard and shouted, Give us
the custody of the little child or I'll do more than
pull out every hair on your head. My grandfather,*

the chief of police, was not a man to ignore. So we came home, Malika and I, but still I was very ill. Malika was taken from me, and placed in the care of my auntie. Her mother's gone mad, they said, she's gone mad with grief, and she cannot look after her child. And they found me a place with the Sisters, in an asylum where I stayed more than twenty years.

The nuns were kind and gentle and from my room I looked out at pine trees, where doves nested throughout the year. I asked for nothing but solitude, for quiet to remember the past, to remember the three years of our marriage and the happiness I had known.

"Maman, Maman." Hind shouted almost as soon as she'd returned to her grandmother's room. "Maman, Teta's fallen from her chair. Come help her, Maman," Hind cried, as she rushed to the kitchen to find her mother. "She was sleeping when I came to lunch, Maman. Now she has fallen down."

Malika followed the child back to the room, then sank on her knees at her mother's side, lifted the old woman's limp hand and held it to her face.

"Is she dead? Maman, is Teta dead?"

"Yes, I think so," Malika answered and her voice opened. "Oh, Hind. It is so very, very sad. She's left us just when we'd found her again," and her eyes filled with tears. "Oh poor mother, you were still young. My poor, poor mother." Then she looked again at the stricken child. "Your grandmother loved you very much, Hind. And at least with us she had three good years."

Then Hind's face flushed and she swallowed carefully. "Maman, Teta's box is under her bed. She'll need it now, won't she?" she said, and then she bent her head and cried.

LOVELY TITS

"Come on. I'll help you if you want." Rana grinned. She was lively, shiny, like her curly dark hair. And she was a gorgeous shape. So he didn't really mind that she was also saying he was hopeless, the kind of guy who didn't have the gumption to buy a Barbie doll for his kid.

"Yeah. I'd appreciate it. She's been on at me for months."

They were still sitting in her office, sorting out the last bits of paperwork. Two software companies, no longer talking via e-mail, but talking face to face.

"Difficult, is it? Hmmm . . ."

"No, it shouldn't be. I guess I just couldn't be bothered." That was more honest than he'd meant. He sucked his teeth and could feel the stiff hairs of his mustache stub into his bottom lip. "I like business trips to be business trips, home to be home." That sounded better, reasonable. But she swiveled round in her chair, gave him a piercing look, then shrugged. Clearly, she didn't think much of his answer.

"I don't quite understand. Who asked you to bring back the Barbie, your wife or your daughter?" The teasing note had gone and she looked at him intently.

"Now it's both of them. First, it was Hawa—that's my wife. She had a Barbie doll when she was little. She still has it, but it's tatty and she wants a new one for Aliyah. That's my daughter, she's nearly five. Anyway, Hawa got out her Barbie for Aliyah and now it's all they talk about." He could feel the prickles of his mustache again. He must stop screwing up his face. It probably looked anxious, and certainly wouldn't be good for business.

"Okay, but does that mean you couldn't be bothered for your wife's sake, or for your daughter?" Her question made him uncomfortable, but he couldn't help being impressed. She didn't let anything slip past. No wonder she was a good systems analyst. But not very Syrian. Maybe growing up in Britain made her more relaxed. And direct. He wasn't used to working with a woman like Rana. Actually, he didn't know anyone like her, and he wasn't used to working with women, period. He was out of his depth.

"To be honest, it's a chore I can do without. Aliyah's wonderful, but I feel I hardly know her. I guess I've traveled too much." He felt a twinge of resentment as he said it. They were awfully alike his daughter and his wife. Quiet, pretty, and unpredictable. Unforgiving when he didn't get things right.

"And your wife?"

He looked at Rana. He was tempted to say something about how stiff and demanding Hawa could be. But he checked himself. It wouldn't be fair. "She's a good woman, and a good mother."

"I see," Rana said, and he felt a bit of a shock. Just what did she see, he wondered, and peered at her carefully.

"Come on, then. Let's get this finished and I'll take you off to Toys 'R' Us."

He'd never been out of the center of Oxford, so the ramshackle buildings near the Railway Station came as a surprise. No spires, none of that antique stonework, only scruffy Victorian brick. She suggested they walk, that it would do them good. When they reached the bridge over the Thames, she stopped and leaned down, enthusiastic, almost as if she wanted to dive into the swift gray river. Then she paused and looked out at the bank. "I like those allotments," she said. "All that effort lavished on those tiny plots."

"Hmmm . . ." was all he could say. He'd never thought about allotments before, indeed he'd had to ask Rana what they were.

"And look over there. It's nice the way the woods rise up behind them. Especially when the air is so clear." She nodded at the boiling white clouds which had just drenched Oxford in rain and hail and had now caught the sun and were now rolling away toward the horizon. "Great, huh?" she asked. All he could do was nod, he didn't know what to say about clouds either.

She chattered on as they walked down the road. "I hate those push chairs, don't you? Those stupid women who shove their kids off the curb first when they're trying to cross the road. And the space capsule covers. Poor kids. Crap visibility, no wind on their faces and their mothers don't even have to talk to them once they're inside. Sensory deprivation, really. It's not hard to work out why the English turn out to be way they are."

He listened to her and looked at a lumpy woman pushing the child chrysalis. He liked what Rana was saying. It was sharp and funny. She was so different from

Hawa who was, the thought suddenly came to him, like a
sweet semolina pudding.

"This could be a very tacky adventure," Rana said as
they walked through the car park toward the warehouse
of a building. "The name alone is bad enough. It's seriously naff, don't you think?"

"Naff?" he'd had to ask. Rana's Arabic was laden with
English slang, and his vocabulary just wasn't up to it.

"You'll see," she said, and added as they marched
past the shopping trolleys, "Do people really buy that
many toys in one go?"

They were hit by the smell of plastic when they entered the store, though Rana didn't comment on that.
She'd spotted some Barbie stuff straight away. "Yuk,
paper dolls," and she opened the book to show him: roller
skates, perky hats, full breasts covered by various bits of
clothing. "Barbie dismembered. Great for fetishists." She
rolled her eyes salaciously, "What do you fancy? Gloves
or shoes?"

Gloves he didn't know about, but he thought of the
rack of shoes Hawa kept in her wardrobe. All those
pointy feet, high arched, ready to dance, going nowhere.
He couldn't remember when he and Hawa had last
walked anywhere. Even in Damascus which could be a
wonderful place for a stroll. And they certainly didn't
walk in Jeddah. No one did. And as for dancing . . . He
was glad his glasses were tinted, hoping they hid his
eyes, and his näiveté.

Rana cornered a young lad who was stocking shelves
and asked for the Barbies, and headed off to the back of
the store. He stumbled behind her, glad she was taking
charge.

"Oh, my God! Just look." No grin on her face this
time. She looked dumbfounded, staring at a wall of
bright pink boxes about thirty feet long and twelve or fifteen feet high. When she'd recovered, she smiled ruefully. "Well," she said, "I hadn't bargained for this. So
what kind of a Barbie are you supposed to get?"

"I don't know." But he now understood why Hawa had insisted he buy the damned doll in Britain, not in the Duty Free in Dubai. He'd looked in the airport, but there were only a couple of dolls to choose from. Did Hawa know it would be like this? She certainly didn't know much else. Her world didn't extend much beyond their apartment in Jeddah and her circle of friends in Damascus. Somebody must have told her. She was good at taking other people's advice.

"How about this one?" Rana had spotted a life-sized Barbie wrapped in cellophane like the chrysalis kids. "'You can wear Barbies' clothes too,'" she parroted and gave him a wink. He peered at the doll. About three feet tall, just like Aliyah, but the doll's head was small in proportion to its body, a miniature woman, not his chubby little daughter. "It's grotesque, isn't it? Reminds me of veal crates." Again he had to ask for an explanation, and the way Rana described the factory-farmed calves being shipped off to slaughter left him feeling somewhat sick.

"Actually, she looks a bit like Hawa—my wife," he said, remembering the wedding photos taken in Damascus five years before. Later Hawa had told him she'd hated her makeup. "It wasn't me at all," she'd said, still aggrieved months afterward. At the time he hadn't known better—in fact, he still wasn't too sure what 'me' she was talking about. Anyway, she'd had a chance beforehand to see what "full makeup, applied by a professional," would look like. "Every one does a make-up rehearsal," she'd said, so he'd assumed that she'd been pleased with the result. But she had looked bizarre. Her face was stiff and pale. Like the bisque doll his mother kept in the glass-fronted cupboard. Or a corpse. That's what he'd thought at the time. Strange and comic. Her bright red mouth shaped like a perfect heart. Meant to be romantic, he'd guessed, but it made him feel like a pervert. When he'd collected her from her mother's for the *arada* procession—when he'd first seen her dressed as a bride, he'd been shocked. And, sitting next to her in the back of the decorated car, he'd wondered how he'd manage to kiss the waxy red mouth of her death mask face.

"Really?" Rana brought him back to Oxford. "Really? Your wife must be beautiful, beautiful in that perfect Damascene way." He nodded. Hawa was beautiful, everyone said so. But as he peered at the life-sized Barbie with her wide eyes and simpering smile, he knew nobody could have a mouth like that. It didn't take any account of muscles and bones. He turned away, embarrassed that he'd mentioned Hawa, wondering if Rana had heard it as a jibe.

He looked down the bright pink row of boxes. It was a hateful color. Sick pink, he used to call it when he was a kid. It reminded him of the cotton candy they would buy during the Feast at the end of Ramadan. Vile colored stuff which he'd thrown up on his shoes one year. He felt he was standing at the bottom of a nightmare with pink canyon walls looming above. He wanted desperately to get out, but Rana was showing no signs of unease. She was marching up and down the aisle, calling out the different Barbies he could buy, laughing at the lot of them, not caring who heard.

"Dear god, Look! There's even a Mermaid Barbie with a Swan." Rana was pointing to the lurid green fish tail which glistened through the cellophane of the box.

"She looks like the belly dancer we had at our wedding," he said, trying to get away from Hawa, wanting to make a joke.

"Oh, no! Really? You had a belly dancer at your wedding?"

"Sure, a belly dancer at a wedding makes everyone happy. Part of the show." His cousin Walid had done all the arrangements, so that, as Walid had said, he could relax and enjoy the reception. "The Meridian recommended the dancer, but we had to sort out what she'd wear."

Rana was looking at him very strangely.

"You know, in Damascus the dancers are pretty well-covered, but I wanted one Egyptian-style." More or less naked, is what he had said to Walid. "We like Egyptian dancers in Jeddah. There's a joke about less being more," he added, and then wished he hadn't.

"Oh, so a good belly dancer can do her stuff at the end of a dog's tail? Yuk. That's what I'd call 'naff,'" Rana said, putting her index finger to her mouth. He wondered if her gesture meant something obscene. "I guess I'm one of those people who think a belly dancer ruins a wedding," she added, as if just stating a fact. She wasn't trying to put him down. "Anyway, you're right. This god awful mermaid is a grown man's fantasy completely."

"So what do you know about men's fantasies?" He tried to make it sound light, but he wondered what she did know about men. More than Hawa, he suspected. Rana wasn't married and she hadn't mentioned a boyfriend either.

"Oh, come on, you Syrian-Saudi creep. Even you must have heard about feminism. It's been around for years. Barbie is 'Woman as Sex Object, Exhibit No. 1.'"

Khara, shit, he thought. He wasn't exactly sure what a creep was, but he could guess. And he wasn't used to being talked to this way, and certainly not by some snippy woman. He hated it when people talked about feminism. It made him feel as if he were to blame. But Rana didn't act like a tank, nor was she heavy and graying like Nawal el-Sadawi. But then, maybe he'd never met a real feminist before. And whatever a creep was, he wasn't as bad as she thought. His grin felt tight, but at least he'd managed not to screw up his face.

After a moment, he looked at her again. She had a great body. Then, suddenly, he remembered the first week of his marriage. It was a time he mostly tried to forget. Of course, Hawa had been very young. Nineteen, she'd just finished her bac. And she'd grown up in Jeddah too. That was partly why they'd got together. Damascus was so easy and open, it would have been impossible if he'd found a Syrian girl who didn't understand how they lived in Saudi and who didn't know how housebound she'd be. Hawa's mother was a *muhajjabah*,

veiled. That probably accounted for some of it too. And
Hawa was the oldest, didn't have any big sisters who
might have told her the score. The list of reasons could
go on forever. He felt a flush seeping up his neck.

"Sex objects," Rana continued. "Not one of these
damn dolls looks like it could do any real work. Do you
see Barbie the electrician, or even Barbie the secretary?
And not many computer experts among them either,"
Rana gleeked, flashing him a toothpaste smile. He
wanted to tell her to shut up, but she was too damned
quick. She made him feel like a fool. "Not one of them
shows a lick of creativity either. Sex for security, that's
what it's about, or Stepford wives. Take your choice."

"Look. I've had enough," he said and he could hear
the anger in his voice. "Let's chose a doll and get out of
here." He made a grab at one of the boxes. Rana looked
at him in surprise, then softened and laughed. At herself,
not him.

"Sorry. I've come on a bit strong." She shook her
head and then put her hand on his arm. He was startled
by her touch and his anger got lost in an embarrassing
rush of pleasure.

"It's okay," he grunted. "I just hate shopping." And to
show willing he forced himself to ask about the Stepford
wives. Either her explanation about the movie and the
women who became perfect housewives after they'd had
their brains removed, or perhaps the lingering warmth
on his arm, unsettled him again and he wandered some
distance down the aisle. She was right, of course. But actually the Barbies weren't doing anything different from
what Hawa did every day. Got up, put on her makeup,
did her hair, worried a bit about breakfast, got Aliyah up,
did Aliyah's hair, and got Aliyah to nursery school. That
was pretty much it.

He peered into the "Barbie at the Beach" box, Barbie
and her beach shower. It made him realize he'd never even
seen Hawa in a bathing costume. In fact, he was pretty
sure she didn't have one. It had never before occurred to
him to ask whether or not she could swim. Probably not,

he concluded. She wasn't very good at being more or less naked. He felt himself starting to redden again.

Their wedding night wasn't the problem, what happened then didn't count. Walid had wanted him to relax, but by the end he'd been so exhausted he could barely recognize the guests as he and Hawa walked around the ballroom arm in arm. And if he'd been that tired, he could only guess what Hawa had been feeling. Throughout the reception she'd sat bolt upright on the wedding throne, staring down from the *eski* glassy-eyed, pale like a mannequin. The huge backdrop of carnations, hearts, and doves picked out in red and white, had looked more animated. And when they'd finally taken the elevator up to the bridal suite, she'd mumbled something about having been sewn into her dress. He'd have to be careful, she said. It would be difficult to get off. In the end, neither of them had taken off a stitch, they'd just collapsed on the bed and fallen asleep. He couldn't be sure if he'd even removed his shoes.

"I take it all back," he heard Rana say from the other end of the aisle. "Here's Barbie with a piano. But come and have a look. It's called 'Two in one—sofa chair and piano,' and guess what? Barbie's reposing decorously on the sofa, in case you expected her to be playing a Chopin étude." He came up and had a look, and saw too the mischievous sparks in Rana's eyes. She'd started again. Perhaps she couldn't help herself, but she made him smile. She was talking to him, trying to get through. And he had to admit that a part of him enjoyed being teased. He could take it, he thought, and decided to find another Barbie doing something.

"Rana," he invited her down to the mouth of the canyon to look at Barbie the horsewoman. 'Barbie with Allegra, who whinnies when Barbie rides. I whinny,' said the vomit pink box.

"Wow!" He wasn't sure whether she was pleased he'd picked up her challenge or just mocking him.

"Ah. Pony Club clits," she said, then saw he didn't understand. "Little girls' porn. The perfect Arab with a flowing white mane. A real nightmare," Rana added in English, then looked at him and muttered, "It's a joke."

"And look at the next one," Rana pointed. "'Champion.' Jet black. What a stud!" Then she paused a moment, her smile vanishing. "A bit racist, what do you think?" He didn't know what to think. He was working hard just to keep up with her. And he wasn't very sure what was sarcasm and what was not. Barbie and the horse's saddle were covered in red tartan. "Dressage. Discipline. So how would you fancy Barbie with a whip?" Rana was beginning to frighten him. He didn't know what to say.

"Does your wife ever come with you on your business trips?" He looked around, wondering what had provoked her question. Not that he could avoid it, now that she'd asked.

"Sometimes. When I go back to Damascus. We can't afford it otherwise. And who'd look after Aliyah? Anyway, I'm not sure Hawa's that interested in traveling. She's embarrassed about not knowing English and worried she'll make stupid mistakes."

"That's a shame. Maybe it'll be different when Aliyah's older."

"Maybe." But he couldn't see it.

At this point they stumbled onto the few Kens in the collection. "Dishy, huh?" Rana laughed. "'Ken is scented with flower fragrance.' That's good, isn't it? But they haven't even given him real fake hair, only molded plastic. No body hair either," she said, and looked appreciatively at the thick black wires on the backs of his hands.

What was this woman up to? She was too nice to be playing the whore. But he couldn't help it. He felt a stirring, a throb of desire. This could get tricky, he thought and started to back off down the aisle, but he had to give in and laugh when she pressed her thumb gently against Ken's cellophane and shorts and shouted gleefully, "No genitals either. But then what did we expect?"

It wasn't the wedding night, but the next few days that upset him. They'd had a local honeymoon. A week in Malula before he'd had to return to Jeddah. And yes, he had balls and a prick in good working order. But what was he supposed to do, rape his wife? Maybe that's what some men did, but it wasn't his style. So there'd been four agonizing days of trying to help Hawa relax, enjoy being touched, kissed, and not so damned shy. Okay, maybe he had been like a stranger. They hadn't had much time together even though they'd been engaged for a six months. Believe it or not—it still made him angry—as a Saudi citizen he'd had to wait that long for permission to marry. And most of that time she'd been in Damascus preparing her trousseau and getting the wedding dress made. But it was as if she'd never heard that a man's pajamas are not the same as his tie. Why, during those six months, had she avoided finding out about sex?

Well, that wasn't strictly true. She had found out something, or, maybe it was instinctive, he didn't know. When they'd finally managed to deal with the virginity problem, she'd started complaining, timidly, he'd had to admit, about being sore. Then her headaches had started. And then Aliyah had come along—right away, and things hadn't been a lot better in the whole five years.

But maybe it was just him. He didn't know. He was startled to hear himself give a deep huffing sigh. Blushing, he looked up quickly, and was glad to see Rana some way off down the aisle.

"Yo, look!" she called. Reluctantly he joined her. He was feeling battered. "Cross-cultural Barbies. Italian Barbie, Kenyan Barbie. Chinese Barbie and like them all 'Made in China.' But, no Arab Barbie. Shall we try and guess why?" She paused, waiting for an acknowledging nod.

'My hunch is that they think that genuine, authentic—that is to say, Arab folkloric—dress would hide too many of Barbie's charms. After all," her voice sharp with sarcasm, "we know that all Arab women—who are all Muslims, of course, never atheists, Christians, or Jews . . . that all Arab women wear black cloaks with just a tiny peephole for their seductive, singular eye."

Rana was getting wound up. It made him want to squirm, made him worry that she was going to be violent. Feminists were often violent, weren't they? Then he checked himself and pulled in his panic. If he made himself listen, she made sense. And how could he blame her? He didn't have to be a feminist to understand. She was good at her job, he admired her for that, and for how well she handled being an Arab woman in an office of Englishmen in Oxford. No wonder she was annoyed.

"Let's just choose one and leave," he said quickly. "I'm grateful you came, but let's get this over and find a cup of tea?" She nodded. This time she had understood. "So which one? You choose. Frankly, to me each one seems as good—or bad—" he wanted her to know he wasn't a complete creep, "—as the next."

Rana walked soberly between the towering boxes. "If they have been waiting a long time for this Barbie, why don't you go for bust and take the Barbie bride. After all, as it says on the box, 'She's got something special. This is the day Barbie has dreamt of so long. She's a vision in her glorious bridal gown.'" Rana suppressed a giggle, then looked at him contritely.

"That's a good idea." Then he paused, still trying to match Rana's sardonic style. "I don't think we'll bother with Ken, do you? After all, there's no Ken in a bridegroom's dress."

Rana laughed. She was nice. "Yeah, let's grab a few button and bow accessories and get out of here," but she couldn't resist commenting on the next aisle down from the Barbies which was chock full of Action Men, Night Climbers, and one Ninja Turtle after the other, each more murderously ugly than the one before. "Yuk," she said and looked so dispirited that he wanted to reach out and say they aren't the worst things in the world. But he didn't, partly because he didn't dare, and partly because she was right. The toys were revolting. And maybe they did say it all.

As they started to walk back, the bridal Barbie boxed in, swinging sideways in a huge plastic cocoon, Rana said, "There is a lovely footpath along the east side of Osney Island which goes all the way over to Christ Church. Do you think we can cleanse our souls with some fresh air?"

The Thames was close and high as they walked along the row of small brick houses. They paused at the bridge near the weir, watching a swan, sans mermaid, struggle against the current. "So when do you go back to Saudi?"

"Tomorrow evening."

He looked out to where the sun was setting behind one of the little warehouses which, Rana had quipped, were all that remained of pre-electronic Oxford. "Rana, I've enjoyed these last couple of days. The work has been great. And it's been good to get out this afternoon. I'm embarrassed to say it," he made an effort not to screw up his mouth, "but I've learned a lot. Could you bear to have dinner with me tonight?"

She looked at him, thoughtful, her eyes narrow, her chin tilted up.

"I know I'm still a Syrian-Saudi creep," he smiled as he said "creep" carefully in English. "And of course, you've already guessed that my wife doesn't understand me." He finished, then looked up quickly, relieved to see that she understood he'd meant the last bit as a joke. Though it didn't sound all that funny after he'd said it. He started to suck his teeth. "Anyway, I'd like to talk some more, before we get back to e-mail only.'

"Sure," she smiled. "I'd enjoy dinner. And it'll give me a chance to ask you what you think you're doing for your daughter."

HYENA'S PISS

The party had been great, terrific. And Yasir had been a success. It was late, or rather very early, when one of Reem's friends dropped him off at the corner. He liked her crowd. They knew how to enjoy themselves. And they knew how to get on in the world. The car was pounding with music as Reem's friend drove away and Yasir wove down the pavement toward home.

It had been a theme party, with jungles of twining bodies. A party like those Yasir had only heard about before. Men who were less daring, like Yasir, had worn safari suits and camouflage greens, while others, designer shirts open on hairy chests, stalked slender women who winked cat eyes, and purred and shook great leonine manes of highlighted hair. Yasir hadn't quite managed to Tarzan Reem into submission, but it was a good joke and her friends had laughed, satisfied or on the prowl themselves. Then later, white heat, and white noise had forced them to mime like dumb beasts and the villa had become heavy with lust.

Early on, one of Reem's brothers had come over to their table. He was carrying a drink and produced a refill for Yasir with a clap of his hands. "The singer's been paid in dollars, hard currency," her brother said, and then he'd started to talk to Yasir about some kind of deal. He'd been called over to another table before he could fully explain, but Yasir knew it bode well. "It should be quite a night," Reem's brother grinned, then he put a hand on Yasir's shoulder, "Could be as much fun as the Bahraini's party last month," he said leering as he turned away. Yasir watched as the people parted to make way for him, as if he'd used a machete to cross the room.

Yasir felt great. He pulled his shoulders back and ran his hand through his hair. He tried on the elegant, menacing look he'd been practicing all month, then snaked his hand down the fake-fur sleeve which encased Reem's arm. She'd felt his touch, but kept her eyes down, smiling so only a hint of a dimple puckered her custard-apple-round cheeks. When she did this, the come-hither effect made him shiver, almost made him feel shame. The thought of asking her to marry him had been playing in his head, and teasing his balls, for a couple of weeks.

Finally she looked up. Her deep-set, measuring eyes and the heavy line of her brows drew him near and, at last, he found the courage to speak. "Reem darling, I love you. Would you marry me?" Though he couldn't swear she'd actually murmured "yes," as she reached for her glass, one of her long silvered nails caught the gold chain at his wrist. Tugging gently to free her hand, she'd whispered, her breath on his neck, "My brothers like you. I'm sure we can work it out," and she let her hand trail up his arm. What he dared do was press her hand for a fleeting moment. What he wanted to do was thump his chest and give a Tarzan roar.

In front of the big, stone house, Yasir fumbled for his keys. Streaks of gray were beginning to penetrate the cool dark of the night. He knew now this was the hour when drink turns to a hangover which lasts the whole day. He winced, aching to pitch into bed and let his head swim, but he paused then laughed out loud as he let himself in. Deep down he felt good, felt his life was about to take off. He hardly dared believe his luck.

That afternoon when he woke, the sun was blasting the tiny balcony outside his room into molten concrete. Slick with sweat, suffering a thirst unto death, he tried to use the pulsing din in his ears to retrieve the elation of the night before. But it was no good. The heat from the balcony burned through the cover he'd pulled over his head and a single incongruous thought, unrelenting, laser white, forced him to wake. How was he to tell his father about his plans and secure the old man's blessing?

He groaned. There was nothing self-evident about how to deal with his father. The old man continued to walk every day to the office in Firdows, but Yasir reckoned he'd given up on the business some time in the eighties, some time soon after mother had died. Since then, it had been head down and plod, pious hopes and pray. As if the old man had been pared down to the core, his tough skin and the sweet flesh of his life all gone.

His father had draped the good old days in pale golden tulle, then he'd tweak the curtain to offer peepshow glimpses of a world shrouded in dust. His father's favorite sayings like "Here in Damascus, we've been merchants for a thousand years," irritated Yasir, made him feel cold. Not because he wasn't proud of their history. But because, in spite of the fax machine and the computer spread sheets, the old man still clung to his abacus habits and old-fashioned dreams. He understood nothing about moving from electrics to electronics or running a dealership.

"Father, things are changing," Yasir explained over and over, hoping to hone the business to a sharper point. Dealing with foreigners, telling him how they could get import licenses easily if they knew the right sort of people. But his father would only nod, smooth a wisp of hair over his bald patch, and begin some torturous story about Bakelite radios, his long experience, and their good family name.

Maddening and snobbish as the old man could be, he was well-intentioned. Yasir knew that. Before he had fully realized that the business, and the old man, were in a terminal decline, he'd been willing to sit of an evening and chat. But now the old man was crumpling into a guarded old age and, almost as an insult, he'd started giving Yasir work which amounted to no work at all. If Yasir hoped to pull them out of the nose dive before they were ruined, he needed to make new contacts, find businessmen who understood the present lay of the land. Knowing this, what could he say that wouldn't increase his father's humiliation?

Then, just when he had begun to feel helplessly trapped, he'd met Reem. Almost by accident at an engagement party. Yasir was one of the groom's few school friends who was still around, who wasn't working or studying abroad. Live music, lots of drink and probably drugs, though he hadn't known enough then to be sure, the party had been held in a big villa in the oasis. He had spent most of the evening watching the girls in their prick-teasing clothes. Like a fly—eager, persistent, sticky—but wary of approaching until others had had their fill.

Reem must have been watching, seen him hovering, and taken pity on him. "Come over and join me," she'd nodded and he had looked behind him, sure she was talking to somebody else. "You, I mean," she'd grinned. "I've danced too much, I need to sit down." He'd even wondered whether she was drunk. But he'd sat down and she got him talking and that's how it had all begun.

Now that there was Reem, and the promise of her brothers' connections, he found it impossible to spend the evening with the musty old man. It embarrassed him to think of Reem seeing him at home. Indeed, it embarrassed him to be at home. Most evenings he made a point of getting out and meeting people. Networking, long after his father had arranged himself in front of the television with a piece of melon and pot of mint tea by his side. That's what he'd been doing at the party last night, making contacts and making out with Reem. Yasir flinched in the light from the balcony.

So the problem was how to tell the old man about Reem. Just do it, he said to himself, knowing it wouldn't be easy. He didn't want to unsettle the old man or the contacts he'd worked so hard to set up. Practicing what he was going to say, he crept down to the kitchen, then realized that the siesta was over and his father had already gone back to Firdows.

Shaking with relief, Yasir pulled open one of the battered cupboard doors and took out a round of flat bread. He placed it on the table and carefully poured a line of oil across it, sprinkled the oil with thyme and rolled himself a fat cigar of a sandwich. Then, as he waited for the milk to warm, he remembered his one obligation of the day. Tawfic, his elder brother, would fly in from London at eight. "We'll discuss your new ideas when Tawfic has come," his father kept saying, and he made Yasir feel important and that his plans were worthy of respect.

Yasir liked going to the airport; he didn't know anyone who didn't. It meant leaving Damascus in the early evening when the city looked opulent, regal—a golden crucible set against the shadowed flanks of the mountains. And there was the straight, tree-lined road, a green finger pointing toward the austerity of the desert farther east. When he was a small child, he would plead to be taken up to the viewing deck. Now the magic of the airport worked in a different way. If you knew someone who traveled, then you might travel too. People would often leave work early, ostentatiously claiming a trip to the airport as their excuse. Then, in the dingy reception halls, their tangled connections would sort into greetings and farewells of duty or love.

And this time he would be traveling to the airport in style. Reem had arranged for her brother's driver to take him out in the Mercedes. Reem couldn't come herself. He understood that. It wouldn't look right. Still, it was a remarkable gesture, putting the brand-new white Mercedes at his disposal. Seeing Tawfic's face would be a treat. And the car had an added virtue. It would provide him with a chance to tell Tawfic about Reem and ask his advice about approaching the old man.

Not that he was all that comfortable with Tawfic. His bullying brother had become a man who loved the fit of fatherly shoes. But these days Yasir felt more confident and anyway they had to talk. Tawfic needed to know how out of touch the old man had become. And for his part, he needed to know what was happening in London. He needed Tawfic as an active partner abroad. Tawfic was sure to agree. This past year Tawfic had become less demanding, less insistent that he knew best. Or, perhaps, just a bit lazier and more self-indulgent. Yasir couldn't be sure. But whatever it was, it made Yasir feel on top of things. He smiled at himself in the glass of the cupboard door and took a bite from the sandwich.

When the car pulled up at the door, Yasir got in as if to the manner born. As they sped down the highway busy with evening traffic, he felt as if he'd finally arrived. Of course, Tawfic wouldn't be coming alone. His wife, and the two kids, who made Yasir jealous with their fluent, chattering English, would fill up the house this summer. But that would be okay. Tawfic's wife was a quick, heavy woman who talked continuously about her children and made jokes about how difficult it was to get her fussy husband to eat. And she loved to gossip, especially about new couples. He smiled. He'd be happy to provide her with a thrill or two. She was kind enough, Tawfic's wife. Just oh, so predictable and dull. And so conventionally

Damascene that he couldn't imagine how she coped in London. She was exactly the kind of woman he did not want for a wife.

At the airport, Yasir watched a foreigner and his family received as VIPs. Then he remembered Reem pointing them out at some party. The guy had written a book about Asad, his wife was elegant, Damascene. He felt as if they belonged to him as he watched them leave. They were escorted out a side door well before the shoal of travelers, blinking like blind white fish, escaped the customs hall only to be caught in the nets of family and friends.

Finally Tawfic and his lot came through the door. "We can go straight out to the car," Yasir said, feeling urbane, even cocky, as he bundled the kids toward the door.

"What car?" Tawfic muttered, but Yasir just smiled as he waved to the driver. When the car rolled up, Tawfic's eyes widened and went white in the polished reflection. Yasir smiled when he saw his brother exchange an incredulous look with his wife.

"Daddy, is this Yasir's car?" Tawfic's little daughter asked, but before Yasir could answer, the child was silenced by her father's hand on her shoulder. After that, knowing the ride home wasn't a time for questions and answers, they sat behind the driver's flapping ears, chatting about a delay at Charles de Gaulle and how even Air France served plastic food. Then, during what was left of the evening, the old man and his grandchildren held center stage, prolonging, to Yasir's delight, the mystery of the wonderful car.

Late the next morning, Yasir struggled awake, made himself coffee, then went to find Tawfic on the wide balcony which ran along the back of the house. As he walked through the darkened living room toward the French windows, he stepped on a scatter of Legos, then stumbled over a small metal car. He swore softly. The kids had been up early and mined the room with toys. Yasir, angry, wondered why their parents couldn't teach

them to tidy up when they were through. Then he swore
again. The living room stank of urine which was swim-
ming yellow in the red plastic potty behind the door. The
stench, mixed with the sweet-sour smell of last night's
cigarette smoke, made him feel sick. Fleeing to the fresh
air, he found his brother slumped at the balcony table.

Unshaven, wearing a pale *jellabiyyah*, Tawfic
seemed much older now than during the euphoria of the
homecoming. A rush of concern, like that he often felt for
his father, made Yasir pause. Walking through the litter
of toys strewn on the balcony floor, he said, "*Sabah el
kheir*. Good morning," adding almost inadvertently, "God,
this place is a mess."

Tawfic, who'd not looked up earlier, grunted. Then,
as if to keep Yasir from coming closer, he straightened
and began to replace his sleep-swollen look with one
leaner and more alert. Yasir, thinking only of his
brother's haggard appearance, repeated his greeting and
asked solicitously, "You didn't sleep well last night?"

"Oh. Good morning," Tawfic returned, and Yasir
smiled, not hearing the edge in his brother's voice.

"Wouldn't it be better if you swapped rooms with the
children?" Yasir asked. "I've moved to the back of the
house. It's really much quieter here." Having rescued a
doll which was about to topple off, Yasir leaned over the
far end of the balcony and looked down at the two old
women in the neighboring garden. "They aren't very
noisy. They stay indoors most of the time."

"I'll decide which rooms we'll use," Tawfic growled,
his metamorphosis complete.

"Tawfic, I didn't mean to disturb you. But I'd like to
tell you about the car. Or, more to the point, about my
plans to marry." Yasir was so pleased with his own news
and his wonderful Reem, he barely noticed Tawfic's reaction.

"You've told father about these plans?" Tawfic said
without asking Yasir to sit down.

"No, not yet. I wanted to speak to you first."

"Are you going behind his back?"

"No, it isn't like that. I'm worried about father and I don't know what I should say. He'll be concerned about money, of course, and I'm not sure what we can afford." Yasir stooped and began to pick up the crayons before they melted on the balcony tiles. "He's become very secretive, you know." Yasir shook his head. "Things aren't going very well this end, though I'm doing my best to get them moving. But," Yasir opened his hand toward Tawfic as if inviting him to speak, "the other side is that father loves your children, so maybe he'll be pleased. Happy that there'll soon be more grandchildren on the way."

"You think that, do you?" Tawfic looked intently at Yasir. "You think that father'll be pleased with your news?" Tawfic paused. "Well, it's good of you to consider his feelings, but don't you think there's a lot more to it than that?" Tawfic knocked a cigarette partway out of the packet, pulling it free with his teeth. He took his time lighting it, then sent a roil of smoke over the garden. "Since you've bothered to get up this morning, I think it's time we had a talk."

As he bent to collect the rest of the toys, Yasir snatched quick looks at Tawfic. Something was bothering him, had probably been bothering him for some time. But Yasir couldn't imagine what. Again he felt a rush of concern, but this was swiftly displaced by his eagerness to share his plans. Tawfic would like Reem and she'd cheer him up, Yasir thought, slipping into the other chair.

"Now that you're back in Damascus," Yasir said, "we can get the office sorted. Retire, that's what he should do. Perhaps even spend part of each year in London. That way we could both keep an eye on him once we've weaned him away from work."

"Keep an eye on him?" Tawfic had watched mildly when Yasir had attacked the kids' debris on the balcony, but now, suddenly, he bristled.

Taken aback, Yasir gasped and a slurp of coffee caught in his throat. "Yes," he stuttered, half-choking, "don't you think it might be better that way?"

"Keep an eye on him?" Tawfic repeated. "As if you're the one who's been in regular contact, and paying the telephone bill? I've always liked that Egyptian phrase," Tawfic's voice was soft with sarcasm. "Dancing with a ladder; it's so apt in your case, don't you think? But perhaps you think Father hasn't noticed, or that he approves of what you're doing?" Tawfic finished the cigarette and stubbed it out in a seashell. Then he tensed as if getting ready to spring. "And now you're worried about telling him you want to marry some quicksilver piece. You're a man on the make and the woman's the same."

Yasir heard his father roaring in Tawfic's attack. Cringing, he wanted to run, to hide like a small child. Tawfic just didn't understand. He hadn't yet seen the office on Firdows with its rows of yellowed folders, the old man standing before the gas ring brewing coffee for his cronies who'd stop for a game of backgammon or just to chat.

"It's time you listen to me," Tawfic pressed both hands hard on the edge of the table. "You were always a bad lot. And now you've become an ass-licking climber. You make me sick. Damn you and your borrowed car. Did you plan it? Knowing I wouldn't be able to say anything at the airport? Or have you forgotten that decent people don't accept lifts from strangers? *'Ayb*," the word came out like snarling, "or, perhaps you no longer feel any shame?" The force of Tawfic's words drove Yasir back in his chair. He'd forgotten wariness, forgotten how ferocious his brother could be.

Tawfic stood up and, with a quick glance at the old women in the next garden, he jerked his head toward the living room. Yasir knew he had no choice but to turn, routed and in retreat.

Away from the neighbors, Tawfic began again. "So. You've come trailing to me. You ass. You think you've fallen in love. But if that's love, I spit on it. And now the hyena's charmed you and will lure you back to her den. You've been sprayed with hyena's piss." Tawfic paused. Then he looked out toward the balcony. "Everyone in

Damascus knows you're in the thrall of a tart. So do you imagine that father alone hasn't heard the news?"

Yasir, reeling at Tawfic's description of Reem, ignored the thrust of the last remark and whined, "You're jealous. You've always been jealous of me."

Tawfic's face grew wide with rage, but his voice was dangerously soft. "How dare you say that to me? Jealous of what? The sleaze? Your greed?" His gaze ate into the marrow of Yasir's bones. "Her brothers are buying a penis for their ugly sister. A penis with a good family name. And look what they've found. You're so besotted, you don't even know you're being used. They're slimy, *ghaliz*; they've corrupted your soul."

Just then Yasir's sister-in-law entered the living room. Yasir smiled gratefully, feeling immense relief. She'd be his ally. She'd put a stop to Tawfic's spewing anger. Yasir watched her pick her way through the carpet of toys. He smiled again as she paused and looked carefully back and forth between the two men. But then she turned—slowly, deliberately—toward Yasir. "We have two children. And we must consider their future. These people," she hissed, "your velvet friends, they'll sully our name." Her eyes narrowed and she lowered her voice. "By god, I'll break your legs and carry you round on my back, to stop you marrying that girl." Stunned, Yasir looked at his sister-in-law. It was as if she'd been waiting offstage for her cue. But her next lines were improvised, born of fury and scorn. "Even in London I heard about the Bahraini's party. I know all about the man. Drunk, lecherous, out of his mind. Slobbering over the women. Feeling them up. Dirty dancing with other men's wives." She was shaking as she shrieked at Yasir. "How he called them bitches and bastards and then went around the room, pointing at all the guests. 'You owe me a building contract. You, a business loan. You, a driver and car. And you, you bastard, does your bitch-wife know about your mistress and that pretty diamond brooch?' And even in London I heart how he unzipped his trousers and exposed himself. How he took out his penis, waved it

around, and pissed on the men who owed him favors."
"No one could put a lid on that story," Tawfic interrupted
and put a hand out to calm his wife. "It stinks too much."
He was sneering now. "Even the government has been
embarrassed. They've deported him, as I'm sure you
know. The gossip's been to London and back. And every
taxi driver, every old man and woman," Yasir could see
his teeth, "every soul in Damascus knows what those
people are like, and what their patronage means."

"But I wasn't at the party . . ."

"No, but her brothers were."

Yasir started toward the door, but Tawfic roared.
"You think you've been working for the business, doing it
all alone. But you're a fool. You can't even read the accounts. You've become so enslaved by their cars, their
easy money, you can't even see that Father and I are the
ones who've been making the business grow. By God, I'd
crack your bones and eat you, if you hadn't said 'Good
morning' today." Yasir, his mouth gaping, his arms and
clenched fists pressed down at his sides, stared at his
brother. Stared at the executioner who'd slay him, then
walk in his funeral procession.

Tawfic meanwhile remained completely still, measuring the effect of his words. His lips curled. "Thank you
so much for coming to consult about your engagement. It
shows such touching concern." The sarcasm burned
Yasir's face like ammonia. "Perhaps it means that you're
even beginning to think of others, but you've left it too
late. If father's aged, it's not because of the business. And
in case you have any doubts, it's he who's kept us informed. Or did you think a Mercedes could dazzle him
blind?"

Yasir started backing out of the room. When he
reached the door, he stopped and screamed at Tawfic,
"You've always been a bully, hiding behind the old man's
legs." He felt like he'd been kicked in the stomach, felt
like he was going to retch. He'd been trying so hard for
the business, for Tawfic, for the old man. It was so unfair.
They just didn't understand. Tears stung his eyes as he

crashed down the passage, stumbled through the door, and fled.

Out on the pavement, Yasir walked fast. Groaning, muttering, then talking outloud. "I don't deserve this," he said, trying to get a grip on his hurt. "I don't deserve this," he wanted to shout as he walked down the street. He knew people were beginning to stare.

When finally he slowed, the pain began to ease off and anger, deep, suffusing anger, began to take its place. He passed a shop window and caught sight of his reflection. I don't deserve this, he thought, so angry now he wanted to hit out and smash the plate glass. Shaking, he looked again. Designer jeans, an expensive shirt. He looked good. I'll bloody well show them. I'll call Reem. If they didn't want him, he could do worse than be her man.

GHALIA'S WEDDING

The pastry cook wants a cake,
My mother, a bridal dress,
My friend, erstwhile, loves disaster,
My brother, he seeks to impress.

For months, I've been working on my English. And
for months, the silly rhyme has been running on a looped
tape in my head. It's their endless demands which make
it whir. What they all want, each and every one, is that
the wedding—my wedding—be authentic, Damascene,
and stunningly, amazingly new.

Recently, my rhyme has grown a second verse, even
worse than the first.

Oh, it's hard to be a bride,
But I'm doing what I can,
For me the wedding is a way
To leave here with a man.

I like the second verse better. It gives me courage.
Doggerel, dogged courage. It's been a dog of a year.
Though, actually, my English is getting quite good!

It started with the man, of course. Sami, Sam. But
temporarily he's become less important than the rest.
Maybe because he's away, happy to leave the arrangements to me. He's studying in America. He's handsome,
thirty-four, doing his internship, and soon to be a doctor.
He'll be back just for the wedding, then we're off, together, to New York.

He's a nice guy. I'm very fond of him.

An excellent match, they chorus in my head. Aren't
you forgetting, they shout in unison, good family, old
money, a respectable future here.

No, I'm not forgetting. How could I? You remind me
every day?

The colors of their words harmonize like some garish
rainbow, fashioned in bad taste. Mother's pink soprano,
cook's eggy yellow, the bilious greens of jealousy, and the
bass of my brother's ambition, blue-black with eagerness,
emulation, and greed. Then the chord mixes white, my
white, bridal white, the white of fright.

They'll have their spectacle, but it's not going to be me.

Three months to go.

"If I were you I'd cancel the whole thing," Amal sits
toying with her food, then looks at Maha for confirma-
tion. And me—Ghalia? I'm suspended somewhere in between, blown one way by the puffs of Maha's minty
breath, then back again on the stench of garlic from the
clove Amal unwisely bit in two. I've known them both

forever and we were friends doing English at college. We're having an expensive lunch at the Chaumière.

"You wouldn't cancel it, you know," Maha says. Amal tosses her chestnut shiny hair which is so well cut it can take any amount of disruption.

The breeze she stirs makes me nod, emphatically. I agree with Maha. Cancel a Sheraton wedding? Not bloody likely. Amal's trying it out as a joke. Cancel the wedding? She wouldn't. Not unless provoked by more than bad luck. And me? I've been dealing with bad luck. And I've made a good job of it. Getting better at it every day.

"But you know what I mean." Amal bunches up her mouth to give a hint of her distaste.

"That she's so good humored?" Maha's been a loyal friend.

"So good humored, it's unnatural," Amal interrupts. "Like a helium balloon. Nothing seems to get her down."

"She's just pretending," Maha begins again, this time softly, charity in her voice. I watch a tinge of guilt suffuse Amal's sharp, pointy face.

All weddings are *kizb*, lies, I want to say. But they know that anyway. Lies and envy, and judgments. And a chance to poke fun.

"Can you imagine," Amal's brush with guilt passes and she rattles on, repeating my story for the twenty-third time. Dancing to the gossip two-step. She does it very well. Something borrowed, something blue, then something firsthand, if not exactly new. That's not quite what they say in English, but it's what we do here.

"Can you imagine? First your granny dies. And the wedding must be postponed."

"Then Sami's uncle dies. And so it's postponed again. What bad luck, to have it rescheduled twice." Though it's unseemly, Amal smacks her lips. Gossip is like porn; she's turned on by other people's woe. But perhaps I'm unfair, perhaps it's the taste of her crème caramel.

Maha takes up the theme, but in a more kindly way. "Surely these things are written, fated," she says, suggesting a higher wisdom, benign providence.

Amal listens, but the smile which hangs on her face
is like an amulet against a curse.

"But you've made quite a catch." Amal smiles, bask-
ing briefly in my good fortune. "That is, if you ever manage to marry him." She means it as a joke, but sits back
as if to rest her case. Implying trials without number, my
chance of success very slim.

A catalogue of really dreadful things runs through
my head: war, famine, plague, engaged couple in a double suicide pact. It scales down Amal's crocodile concern.
I want to shake her until her teeth rattle and her tears
spill on the floor.

"But of course, in one way you've been lucky. Three
times you've had the fun of planning, when some of us
aren't yet in a position to try."

Maha flinches, bends forward, punched in the guts
of her fear.

A bitch of a remark, deliberate. Maha knows this
and so do I.

And lest either of us misinterpret, Amal waves her
engagement diamond and a sunburst of confidence falls
on the linen cloth.

I feel a slight sting. A pricking sensation—a spark
from the diamond has touched and burned my cheek.
But what can I do? I should be on an emergency ward—
Adrenalin, respirator, electric shock—or perhaps I'd just
give Maha a thump between her shoulders and whisper
'Don't listen, Maha. She's a cow.' The problem is I don't
know how to administer the thump, nor do I dare to
shake Amal, though I'd dearly like to try.

I shrug. Recently, I've become the perfect spy. The
microphone in the carnations, the bug in the bedroom,
the fly on the wall. But I'm struggling for executive
power, struggling to find ways to intervene. It's very frus-
trating, this state of affairs. I see my frustration colored
cooked marrow green. The same shade as Maha's fear
and the color of Amal's spite. Cooked marrow green. But
if I said that, who else would understand?

Two months to go.

"Oh Ghalia. What will people say? What are we going to do?" My mother, like a small brown sparrow, flutters, chittering in her panicky way.

"Ghalia, sit down. There's been some dreadful news."

"Mama, you sit down. Tell me, what's happened now?"

She draws her hands through her straying hair. I comfort her, settle her on a small gilt sofa.

"Mama, tell me." My heart is jumping to my throat.

"Your wedding dress. Your beautiful beaded gown. The dressmaker's . . ." Her voice rises shrill, then collapses in a sob.

"The dressmaker's house . . . ," she starts, then starts again. "The dressmaker's house has gone up in flames."

"And my gown?"

"Gone. Gone up in flames."

Fire. Last night. No one hurt. But our good-hearted seamstress ruined.

Stock-still, I stare at her shaking body, at Mama's streaming face. Frozen, though I wish that I could cry. Then angry, my body thaws. "Oh Mama, I'm tired of disasters," and laughter, hot bellyfuls of laughter billow out in place of tears. I can see myself as the first naked Sheraton bride.

"Oh, Mama," I cradle her head on my shoulder, "poor Mama, your only daughter's jinxed."

"How can you laugh?" She's angry now. "That's exactly what they'll say."

Already I can hear Amal on the phone, using my story to fill her day. "I'm so sorry for the dressmaker. She's done some nice things for me." Then prettily she pauses, the artless ingenue, "Poor Ghalia, it must be such a shock, her wedding dress gone up in flames."

Istamsahna, we're crocodiles, we all become hard-skinned beasts.

I'll give her a shock, I think, wondering what it should be.

"We must help her, Mama. And pay her well, the dress was almost done." Fichu neckline trimmed in lace, puff sleeves, enchanting bow details on bodice, skirt, and train. Now gone, gone up in smoke.

Then suddenly I feel relief. It was a simpering, saccharine dress, now turned to a brulé sweet. And I'm like Baked Alaska, oven hot and icy cold conjoined.

"There's no time," my mother whines. "How can we have another dress made? We'll have go to London," she begins to chatter, "drifting tulle, high necked with Calais lace," another gown already in mind.

I stop her abruptly. There's no sense now in playing safe. I'm twenty-one, the wedding's near, and marriage is the only choice I have. So dammit, I'll be a phoenix; be up and off and on my way.

Then I pause. Brave words, I think. Not quite believing myself.

"Cheer up, Mama. We'll manage something." I'm being tugged to another place. Pulled to the wardrobe, standing ornate and tall in my mother's room. "Mama," I call. "Mama, come."

"Do you still have great-grandmama's *bindola*? Her beautiful dress, is it still here?" a fleeting glimpse from childhood glitters in my eye. "The wine-red gown in tissue paper, folded in its flat wooden box?"

For a moment, my sparrow mother looks at me, curiosity edging to fear. "Oh, you can't do that. You must wear white."

"But great-grandmama didn't."

"Ghalia, you can't wear that dress. Just think what they all would say. That we couldn't afford a second gown, now the first has burned away. Have a *qirsh*, worth a *qirsh*, we'd be the laughing-stock for years."

"Mama, stop! Money may be the nerve of life, but we're not nouveau riche. We don't need to invent a past and wear it new on our backs."

She pauses, then blinks. Gives a jerky little nod.

"Do you really want to wear it?"

"Yes. I'd like to wear her dress."

Comforted, "It will want lots of gold to set it off. Old-fashioned gold, your grandmother's gold." Then she becomes more assured. "Gold, like juice in a jug. There when you're thirsty, there when you have some need."

At the back of the wardrobe, we find the dress, the heirloom, treasure dress. And we admire the gold embroidery which glints full length as I whirl it in front of the mirror.

It wants to be worn, my mother sees that, and she gives up the fight and goes to the kitchen to make some tea.

One month to go.

And oh, there is a lot to think about. Not least the piste. The piste that makes a summer wedding spectacular on the scale of Cecil B. DeMille.

I know what my brother is thinking, and he's dangerous in a thinking mood. Mother, excited, told him about my new old dress. But unwisely, I fear, for since then, his scratchy thoughts have been playing heritage themes.

It's Friday afternoon and we've gone to the Sheraton pool. "A wedding is an investment," he says, "a chance to entertain." He dreams of a wedding that will make a splash. In the eyes of his friends, he means.

I should have been more alert. But I'm inattentive, distracted by the glass of pink lemonade he's balanced on his chest. Next thing I know, he's remembered last year's *houdaj* and my heart sinks in the deep end of the pool.

People say that big weddings are all the same. But they're not. Or at least, everyone tries for something new. Last year the *houdaj* was exciting, at least for a moment or two. A palanquin for the bridal couple who made their entrance sitting side by side.

He's never been very original, my brother. But that's never worried him a bit. In Damascus, they say that when something costs money, there'll be imitations by the afternoon. Apprehensive, I'm watching now as he leans back on the cushioned deck. Like a mountaineer, he studies the staircase which climbs the southeast face of the massive hotel.

First, he conjures up a tented throne, a *houdaj* for a Bedouin bride. Not satisfied, the next is more grand, a *houdaj* for Sallahudin's queen.

I try to stop him. Try to tell him that the couple have been forgotten, what lingers is the memory of a joke. A *hodaj*, swaying, precarious, carried by young men, untrained and out of step: the retreating soldiers from an Omayyid army, extras from a bad historical film.

But he won't listen. Goes on dreaming. Of a *houdaj* carried by camel, across mountains from Acre to Aleppo, deserts from Damascus to Baghdad. And then, even worse. His daydream journeys east and the *houdaj* has become an howdah, with elephants and a mahout.

"Stop," I shout at him. "Even camels are impossible." But I still can't make him hear.

"They didn't dare the staircase. They made their wobbly entrance from the side." I begin to panic and gesture frantically. "You can't bring me down the staircase. Broken legs, broken arms, broken neck. I'd end up a crumpled heap of bride." And then, to my astonishment, the tall glass topples, iced lemonade pours down his front, and his crazy ideas spill away.

Laughing, but determined to press my advantage, I scold him as fiercely as I can. "You see what happens when you plan my wedding without listening to me?"

He growls as I hand him a towel, denying he was serious about the elephants, camels, *houdaj*.

"Don't lie to me," I say with a grim smile. Having saved myself from catastrophe, I feel magnanimous and suggest an arrangement which I know will please us both. "What about your little twin daughters, they'd look wonderful in the *houdaj*, far prettier than me."

One week to go.

And the great artist is still trying to create our cake.

On a stool in the enormous stainless kitchen sits the pastry chef. Heat wraps round his aproned body, I can smell his dripping sweat. His chef's hat droops, mimicking his despair. Annoyed, I want to push the hat until it hangs, lopsided, cockeyed, over his left ear.

Yet again, he's frowning over his photo album. Photos of the cakes he's baked. Four years of cakes. Every size, every shape, with flowers and doves and hearts. But now his reputation has been broken and none of these will do. He's been out-classed by the pastry chef of another of the grand hotels.

"Water and sugar icing," he mutters, "two things that should never mix." But the cake of his rival has been his undoing and it combined those very things. I do understand what he must feel.

Below that cake was a fountain whose water fell back into a huge, shiny tray. And round the edge of the tray rose six slender white pillars, each a yard high. And on these pillars rested a second tray, and on this tray lay tiered rounds of cake as big as cartwheels. And from the cartwheels rose smaller cakes, seven on each side. Two spiral stairs like angel's wings reaching for the sky. And on the top, yet another cake, where a tiny bridal couple stood.

Truly, a magnificent cake.

Now his only ambition is to discover the next most impossible, improbable thing that can be done with a cake. I'm beginning to get very worried.

Forget fountains, I've been whispering for weeks. To insinuate more modest ideas into his head.

Forget spirals, I say. But his cake mania is growing stronger each day.

There's no time now, my patience is running out. I pound my fists on the counter, jump up and down to catch his eye. As he lifts his head, his hat falls to the floor. And when he stoops to recover his crowning glory, I head-butt him with another idea.

"Think tall," I say. And I see a gleam cross his face. "Think tall," I've made some headway at last.

"Tall," I say again. "Tall as a cypress tree. Tall and sparkly," I whisper next. And I know that I have him hooked.

I like the cake I have in mind. I wonder if it can be done.

No more years, no months, no weeks, no days to go. We've done it, we're here, Sami and I, trembling on the brink. We console each other, perhaps kid ourselves, that we didn't want this show. "It's for the parents," Sami says. "And my brother," I add, giving Sami a rueful smile. I'm an only daughter, and he's an eldest son. And they're the ones who have been longing to entertain everyone they know. Close friends, good friends, necessary friends and all the people they owe.

At least we've dispensed with some of the ritual, the bits that few people would see. Our excuse is Sami, he's been away too long, had no time to plan. So no noisy parade, no *arada*, when the groom collects the bride from her home. We're pleased with ourselves as we arrive in the evening light. Sedate, on time, alone in a single car.

Like a secret, we steal through the hotel doors and speed across the polished floor. Mischievous children in the lift, we push the botton for the bridal suite. He looks suave and tall, I'm delighted his jacket is white. He catches my glance. "Our joke," he murmurs, loosens the neck of my cloak and touches my wine-red dress. On the long ride up, we kiss, brush lips, till suddenly I come to my senses. "Careful, my lipstick. You'll have to wait. Only four hours to go."

An army of helpers, well-wishers, troubleshooters are waiting for us in the room. They slick our hair, our cheeks, our shoes, then allow us to inspect ourselves in the long, wide mirror. "Your dress is wonderful," Sami whispers to me and I praise his bridal white. Then like marathon runners at start of a race, we determine we'll finish the course. "Come on, it's time. Almost ten o'clock," Sami takes my hand.

We're led out of the room to find the great staircase, then we cower behind the parapet in awe. Behind us, around us, sheer walls tower up, sand-colored, golden, majestic. Like *Aida* at Luxor, the pylons of Karnak, or a great

Babylonian palace. Then, with the bats and the night birds on the soft warm air, we find the courage to look down.

A caravan of color, small moving dots, the guests arrive at the oasis pool. A gladiola oasis, Zenobia's garden, bouquets as tall as palms. Bouquets which flank the reception line where our parents stand, formal and proud. *"Alf mabruk,"* a thousand good wishes. They smile and shake each hand.

Ten guests at each round table, each one gleaming white. From here, like craters on the moon. A thousand guests, gossiping, watching. Waiting for the wedding to start.

Still in the dark, my body starts shaking. I can feel Sami trembling too. Amal was right, I should have canceled the wedding before it was far too late. The descent will be heart-stopping. A test of our marriage ties. Resolute Sami reassembles our courage, "It's going to be a long night," he whispers a kiss. I nod, bite my lip and pray everything is under control.

A crowd has now joined us behind the ramparts, invisible to the guests below. The banqueting director, the rest of the cast and the teeming video crew. The lights come up, the countdown starts, and a thundering fanfare begins. A startled pigeon wakes and flies from its perch; I wish I could fly away too. I cringe, want to laugh, it's a movie fanfare, from *Rocky I*, or perhaps the theme of the Mediterranean Games. My God, what a *souq melée* of taste.

The *houdaj* is first. *Bismillah ar-rahman ar-rahim.* Eight young men, in braided waistcoats, take the supporting poles. Their arms bulge as they lift the palanquin shoulder high and begin the steep descent. Their first steps are tentative, careful, cautious, their baggy blue trousers, like pennants billowing in the wind. Then they find a rhythm and angle down, tassels bobbing in strict time.

The occupants, my brother's twins, have been strapped in with satin bands. They squeal, then shush each other and sit white-faced in delicate tulle. Braver

soon, they begin to wiggle and their dresses start to froth.
"Sit still," I hear one of the bearers shout. And terrified,
the twins remember their special role and scatter rose
petals in their wake.

Down the great staircase, the spotlight follows.
Slowly, step by step, gladiolas line their way. Then a
pause at the bottom while trumpets blare and the young
men rearrange the load. Across the dance floor, they parade in a stately march, then angle downward again.

The next flight of stairs, the guests have stopped
breathing, waiting for the *houdaj* to reach the berib-
boned aisle. Then the silence is broken, there's even applause. The guests smile at the children as they are
carried by, then brush petals from their glittering
clothes. Thirty yards more and they're at the dais where
the children are helped to dismount. Two grinning girls,
they wave at their father, then settle like cherubs either
side of the bridal throne.

"They've made it," Sami exhales and squeezes my
arm. Not skittered, nor slid, the palanquin has descended
in style. I grin, doubly thankful. So glad I wasn't inside.

Next the torchbearers begin their descent, each one
carrying a flaming liquid pikestaff high. Marching down,
the fanfare again, the eight take up places on each side.
Then eight swordsmen pass down the stairs in the bur-
nished, flickering light.

Then the fanfare again. I grasp his arm and down
the piste we go. While still eagle-high, I hear gasps from
the crowd, stunned murmurs, disbelieving. We slow our
pace slightly, snatch looks at each other and almost begin
to laugh. We are dauntless, audacious, my bridegroom in
white and me in great-grandmama's wine-red gown.

Down past the torches and onto the dance floor, we
kiss, exchange rings, and release two frightened white
doves. Then on to the next stairs, now sure-footed as
ibex, and down through the arch of the swords' shining
steel. I can see faces now. Madam the Minister at a table
left, I catch a glimpse of Amal on the right. Her wide eyes

say we've broken with convention for sure. Then smiling our valor at the beaming guests who can't wait to spread the news about town, we walk on down the aisle to sit on the flower-decked throne.

"We've made it!" I whisper and squeeze Sami's knee. He looks back severely, "Tsk. Propriety, Dear heart. Do you think the cameras can't see?" But I'm careless, now giddy, now drunk on success.

We're brought fruit cordial in a brandy snifter, and struggle to drink from twin straws. Then the kissing begins, our parents, our friends, come up to the bridal throne. Even Sami's cheeks have an apple shine when it's time for the opening dance.

"You've planned things wonderfully. It's all going well," he says as we ebb and flow. And Blue Danube words waltz in my head, I'm pleased he's pleased and I'm delighted we'll be gone tomorrow.

Later greeting each guest, we move round the tables, our escort, his mother, helps us with names.

"What a lovely idea, your beautiful dress."

"Thank you," I glow in reply.

"Not copied?"

"Oh, no. My great-grandmama's dress. She wore it when she was a bride."

Then Amal, Maha, my friends tug at my arms, I'm their hostage for the next dance. "A women's dance," they say, "a *debki* to honor your dress." Step by step, we circle round and then the pace increases. Then faster and faster, we dance with intent, as if we could spread wings and fly. We're dizzy, so dizzy, when the last chorus ends, we stumble into each others' arms. Amal's green dress, her pointy face, her spite, none of it now matters a fig. But I do turn to Maha and whisper "You next," and put my posy in her hands.

"Time for the cake," the Banqueting Director, timekeeper, stage manager, comes over to our throne. He's polite, his dinner jacket comfortably worn.

The opening chords, Mendelssohn's wedding march, echo round the oasis pool. Guests crane their necks.

"Wait here," he says, "I'll nod when it's ready, nod when you should come."

My cheeks redden with waiting as Sami well sees. "What next?" he asks with a grin. "I don't know," I say, "We may both of us be surprised."

Slowly, triumphantly, from out of the wings is wheeled the table which carries the cake. "Ooooohhhh. Aaaaahhhh," I hear all around me, like the children watching fireworks over Jebel Qassyoun. "Ohh," I join them. "Ahh," Sami gasps at the waterfall of silvery stars.

It's tall, taller than a tall man stands. A gleaming tower of white. A giant child's plaything, a nest of boxes, a work of edible art. Fifteen—I count them and so does everyone else—there are fifteen layers to our cake. And from each corner, pointing outward, a lighted sparkler burns, a shimmering fountain of light.

"My God, he's done it!" I almost shout, as Sami and I draw back to stare.

Truly it's the most magnificent cake.

We watch enraptured, till the wedding march fades, till the star showers start to slow. Then we walk forward, place four hands on the hilt and lift the great Damascene sword.

"Wait," the Banqueting Director intervenes before we can make the first cut. Then the music ends, there's a moment of silence, as we stand poised and ready. "Now," he commands. And, as we slice into the lowest tier, an extravaganza of light begins.

Shooting stars, sky rockets bombard the heavens, filling the sky above. Then star burst after star burst, first white then gold, turns night into day during our wedding at the Sheraton hotel.

Exhausted, exultant, exuberant, a crushed tuberose in my hand, next evening we're on the plane. It's true, I keep telling myself, I've done it. I'm am leaving Damascus with Sam.

"But did you know about the fireworks?" Sami asked for the fourteenth time.

"No. I had absolutely no idea."

He heard the exasperation in my voice. "The finale was a complete surprise."

"Ghalia, it doesn't matter." He took my hand. "Be pleased. You've organized the wedding of the year."

But it does matter. At least a little bit. I enjoyed being the perfect spy, I enjoyed being in control.

A glint of sunlight from the wing touches and warms my cheek. I sit up, sobered, then smile. Leaning onto to Sami's arm, I see the Mediterranean below, shining, opalescent, like precious rainbow glass. Dancing, like the fireworks on my wedding cake.

POSTSCRIPT:
THE PIRATES' SOCKS

There are many ways I might have chosen to write up my anthropological research in Damascus. The safest and most conventional choice would have been to write up my fieldwork diaries as an ethnographic monograph on gender and marriage among the Damascene owning class. The least obvious alternative was to write fiction: to write *Dancing in Damascus*.

The impetus to write short stories was complex. In part it stemmed from a wish to reach an audience wider than a purely academic one. This wish came from my anger and exhaustion at countering simplistic, popular

123

stereotypes of Arab or Muslim women and men as funda-
mentalists, terrorists, or both, and from my disgust at
my own and other Middle Eastern scholars' silence during and after the Gulf War (see Lindisfarne-Tapper
1991). The wish to write short stories also came from my
certainty that treating the people I knew in Damascus as
ethnographic subjects would be both inexcusably arro-
gant and patently absurd.

I feared that any ethnography I wrote would omit
too much. I worried that I would fail to describe all that
was familiar about life in Damascus while inadvertantly
making it seem exotic. I might flatten the three-dimen-
sional lives of my friends to two and truncate their stories further in tidy case studies. I felt sure I would lose a
sense of the density and breadth of the city. I also knew
I could not write with ethnographic accuracy about gender and marriage among well-to-do Damascenes unless I
also described their cosmopolitanism in global economic
and political terms. In short, it seemed inevitable that I
would fall into the orientalist trap unless I found some
other way of writing up what I had learned from my
fieldwork in Damascus.

Orientalism and the Debate on Ethnographic Writing

These days there is little mystery about how and
why local voices have been muted in the anthropological
literature. The muting has been a source of considerable
embarrassment and profound epistemological pessimism
among anthropologists. Since the 1970s, it has been clear
that the discipline of anthropology has typically served
the interests of those who are white, Western, and male.

Anthropology as a discursive adjunct to colonialism
and imperialism has been widely discussed (cf. Asad
1973; Said 1979, 1989). The orientalist indictment has
focused attention on the intimate association between
western academic and political establishments. The debate on ethnographic writing has further implicated the
anthropological enterprise of studying the Other (cf.

Clifford and Marcus 1986), while feminists and women of color have provided some of the most cogent political and philosophical critiques of what is now often known as the problematic of social difference (cf. Nicholson 1990; Faludi 1991; Mohanty 1992).

Such critiques suggest that anthropological discourse cannot but reproduce arguments which reinforce difference and ultimately oppression. They have been widely discussed in the anthropology of the Middle East (Said 1989; Moors 1991; Abu Lughod 1993; Lindholm 1995), where the issues have been most keenly exposed during the Gulf War and its dreadful aftermath and where questions of censorship, self-censorship, and the travesties of media coverage are now all too familiar (see Norris 1992; Makiya 1993).

In situations where local voices are muted by orientalist practices, the right to reply has often been pre-empted because the subjects of an ethnography lack formal education or the requisite languages to participate in the academic discussion. But the silence of anthropological subjects is not always a measure of their exclusion. The people with whom I worked with were typically well-educated members of a wealthy elite who spoke Arabic and French, and some of them English, far better than I could. Indeed, in Damascus, I found myself doing what Laura Nader called "studying up" (1969; see also Schrijvers 1991). Yet whatever the educational level or social background of the subjects of fieldwork, another factor—one often willfully ignored by anthropologists—is relevant: almost by definition informants are people who already know in their bones all that can be said academically. After all, every day they live the experiences the anthropologist struggles to describe.

Writing Fiction

When I first realized that I needed a new way of writing about my fieldwork in Damascus, I looked for compromise styles which would both allay my fears and accommodate my new ambitions (see, e.g., Glass 1990; Lieve 1996). I made a number of false starts trying to mix travel writing, journalism and autobiography before I understood that hybrid forms between ethnography and fiction are often tedious and self-serving simply because the main protagonst is the author. I didn't want to write about myself, but I did want to write about the astonishing people I'd met, so I settled down to learn something of the craft of fiction writing. It has been a lengthy and salutory experience.

Fiction and ethnographic writing differ from each other in a number of ways, though never as radically as some anthropologists would have us believe (see Carrithers 1988). Fiction derives its narrative force from immediacy and suspense. It challenges both writer and readers to explore their assumptions about human nature. Ethnographic writing describes in detail the social relations already outlined in the introductory pages of a monograph, thus flattering both writer and readers by encouraging them to partake in a subject in a knowing way. Good fiction writing depends on a recognizable aesthetic and honest characterization, while much of the authority of ethnographic writing derives from a distanced account of the unfamiliar. Most importantly, each genre has a distinctive relationship with its audience: more consensual in the case of fiction (fiction readers will simply close a book if not they are not emotionally engaged) and more authoritarian in the case of ethnography (ethnographies are often dry and obscure almost certainly because those who read them—students, teachers or professional anthropologists—have to read them as part of their work).

In the case of *Dancing in Damascus*, the question of audiences drove my story writing and most clearly informed my understanding of fictional styles and values. The stories of *Dancing in Damascus* have been written for several overlapping sets of readers. Part of my intended audience is unsurprising. I have written the stories for my students, academic colleagues, and a wider public reading in English, among them those who travel, work, or live in the Middle East. Less expectedly, from the outset I have also intended the stories to be read by Syrians, in English and in an Arabic translation. Anthropological fieldwork is not often written up explicitly for a local audience, though many accounts of anthropological advocacy (see Wade 1995) and ethics (see Pels 1996) recommend that it should be. The implications of such a choice are worth exploring.

Read in English or Arabic, the success of the stories of course depends on my ability to write within the genre. For those who know Damascus, my sensitivity (or lack thereof) as an anthropologist is revealed in the degree of the stories' emotional and descriptive accuracy. In spring 1996, shortly after I had completed *Dancing in Damascus* in a first draft form, I took them to Damascus to Syrian friends who had offered to read the stories and share their comments and criticisms with me. The response I got was beyond all my expectations and one of the most exciting events of my anthropological career. Friends discussed and debated the stories from inside, identifying themselves with the protagonists, comparing experiences, angered or amused by what I had described. Then Mamdouh Adwan, the Syrian poet and playwright, agreed to translate *Dancing in Damascus* into Arabic and to my enormous pleasure *Al raqs fi dimasq* appeared in 1997 (see Lindisfarne 1997b). Elsewhere I am writing about the reception of *Al raqs fi dimasq*. Here my aim is to raise more general issues about doing field research, accountability, and writing anthropology as fiction (see Lindisfarne 1997c, 1998). Indeed, this postscript is, in effect, an extended discussion of my relationship with my Syrian audience during the fieldwork period itself.

The Road to Damascus

I first visited Damascus for a few days in the summer of 1966. My then husband Richard Tapper and I were traveling to Iran to do anthropological fieldwork in

Azerbaijan. We arrived in Damascus at night, having driven there from Beirut; I remember vividly seeing men robed in white *jellabiyah*s sitting under the neon lights of the cafés along the Barada River. We stayed in the big government hotel, also near the river, but on the main road closer to the city center. Huge willows lined that road whose soft asphalt was strangely cross-hatched. I'd never seen tank-tracks before and I was both shocked and excited.

Richard and I visited the *souq el Hamidiyyah,* the covered bazaar, and we stopped for a long time in a musical instrument shop watching a man repairing an *aoud,* a great, fat-bellied Arab lute. I played the guitar then and wished afterward I had bought an *aoud.* But they were expensive and it would have been impossible to transport such a delicate instrument to Iran and back safely in our already laden car. Afterward I often wished we had an *aoud* at home to add an Arab dimension to the musical world of our two sons who were born some years later. From my first visit to Damascus, the only other memory which remains so clear is of the size and silence of the Great Omayyid Mosque.

I did not return to Damascus again until the summer 1988 when I hoped to begin anthropological fieldwork on families and marriage in an urban setting. My sons, then young teenagers, came with me that summer and for two weeks we traveled widely in Syria, exploring the country as tourists while canvassing opinion on where I might best settle. In the end, the decision was easy. I wanted to work in Damascus, among people living in some unexceptional lower-middle-class neighborhood where I might improve my spoken Arabic and pursue my study through the classic anthropological method known as participant-observation.

Over three extended visits which together lasted some eleven months, I completed my field research in Damascus. Coincidentally, my fieldwork drew to a close in August 1990, just after the Iraqi army invaded Kuwait. Since then, I've been back twice, in 1993 and 1996. The stories of *Dancing in Damascus* are set in 1989 and 1990, during the period I was there. Later Syria joined the group of "the allies" opposed to Saddam Hussain and afterward became one of the Gulf War winners. The state-controlled economy was opened up to private business and tourists began to feel safe and welcome in a country which had been viewed previously with relentless hostility by Western governments.

Two Stories, First Fictions

When I began my research I had no thought of writing fiction. However, soon after my sons returned to England, Abu Riyad, the father of my close friend, Hazar, told me two stories. Both stories were about men and armies, arrogance and power. I now think my interest in storytelling dates from that time.

In the Arab world parents are often known by the names of their eldest children, but the custom surprised me when I met Abu Riyad: partly because I'd forgotten about Riyad, Hazar's elder brother who lived in France, and partly because the name seemed too casual for Abu Riyad who was tall, graceful, and silver-haired. He'd recently retired, Hazar explained; he was one of the best-known doctors in Damascus.

When first we met, Abu Riyad greeted me in English with great courtesy. After he'd asked me a series of questions about my proposed research, he paused. "There's a story I'd like to tell you." His voice changed and he spoke with all the flourish and formality of a *hakawati*, a traditional storyteller. I was immediately alert.

Sallahudin and Richard the Lion Heart

"One day," Abu Riyad began, "after many battles, and having been enemies for many years, Sallahudin and Richard the Lion Heart finally met face to face. And when they met, they saw that they were indeed worthy competitors. 'Enough of fighting,' Sallahudin said, 'Let's settle what's between us like true warriors, with swords, in a single contest.'

"Richard agreed, and the two kings sharpened their finest blades and the next morning at dawn they met on the flanks of Jebel Qassyoun. And there they drew lots and it fell to Richard to begin. With the first stroke of his mighty broadsword, he cut down a small tree level with the earth. Then Sallahudin, with his sword of Damascene steel, matched Richard's blow, and a second tree fell, ready to be turned into kindling wood.

"Richard, greatly disturbed by what he'd seen, raised his sword and clove a thick iron bar in two. He stood back, sure that he had won. However, Sallahudin, without a moment's pause, raised his shining weapon and with two quick strokes, divided the iron bar twice again.

"Richard, in fear of losing, hurriedly looked around and seeing nothing else, he smote a great stone. Though a crack appeared across the face of the boulder, his sword shattered and fell in pieces at his feet.

"Then Sallahudin, his white teeth flashing under a heavy beard, took the fine silken scarf from around his waist and tossed it in the air. With a cut so swift that the eyes of the generals who were watching their kings could barely follow the movement, Sallahudin divided the silken cloth midair. Catching both pieces before they touched the ground, he handed one to his opponent.

"Richard, vanquished, accepted the piece of silk and bowed to Sallahudin."

At first I didn't understand Abu Riyad's parable. Later I realized he meant the story as a cautionary tale. He was chiding me not to presume about either East or West. It was a signal start to my fieldwork in Damascus, fieldwork for which I was, in theory at least, well-prepared.

Doing Middle Eastern Anthropology

Several related themes—gender, Islam, and the politics of marriage—had been of continuing importance in all my previous anthropological research. In the mid-1960s, in Iranian Azerbaijan, I'd done a study of women's gatherings among pastoral nomads known as the Shahsevan. Five years later I began a second field study among pastoral nomads in northern Afghanistan which focused on marriage as a means of managing political and economic competition. A decade later, I was fortunate to study aspects of practiced Islam in the town of Eğridir in southwestern Turkey. Then, in 1987, I became a lecturer in anthropology of the Arab world at the School of Oriental and African Studies, University of London. I studied Arabic full-time for a year with the expectation that I would do further anthropological fieldwork, this time in the Arab Middle East.[1]

Before I began my field study in Damascus, I already knew a fair amount about gender issues, marriage, and wedding ceremonies in the Middle East. Yet there were only a few ethnographic studies of Syrian communities (see, e.g., Rabo 1986), although happily there were several early accounts of the institution of marriage (see Chatila 1934; Daghestani n.d; *Taqalid al-zawaj* 1961). Perhaps more surprising, given that over half the population of the Middle East now lives in cities, there were few anthropological or sociological monographs about the lives of people of the urban middle classes (on Damascus, see, exceptionally, Terjuman 1978/1995). Although I did not understand its consequences until later, filling in these gaps created another impetus toward fiction: the liveliest and most vivid accounts of domestic life in Damascus were to be found in novels, short stories, and a variety of autobiographies and fictionalized autobiograpies written by Syrian authors, and widely known in Damascus.[2]

My preparations for fieldwork in Damascus were as thorough as I could make them, yet I did not anticipate the direction my study would eventually take. As

Bernard Cohn has pointed out in his careful and amusing comparison between anthropologists and historians (1987), anthropologists create their own data through fieldwork. It is an exercise whereby the anthropologist first defines what kinds of information will tell us most about social life in a particular setting, and then decides how best to acquire this information in a systematic and disciplined manner. Yet, paradoxically, one criterion for judging good fieldwork is the degree to which the fieldworker has been responsive to what is new and unexpected. Local preoccupations should always determine the focus and style of an anthropological study. Sometimes the local influences which shape a study are gradual and all but invisible; sometimes, as for me in Damascus, they are not.

The Politics and Poetics of Everyday Life

My friend Hazar was responsible for the strength of many of my earliest, most abiding impressions of Damascus. Although a description of her verve and black humor would not fit easily into a conventional ethnographic monograph, it was she who first raised questions about gender and the state which have haunted me ever since. It was from Hazar too that I first learned of the particular Damascene form people's sense of injustice and indignity took. How this anger fit with other aspects of people's lives became for me an important question. It is one of the central themes which unite the stories of *Dancing in Damascus*. Hazar and I had been flatmates at college in London and stayed friends for twenty-five years. "Come to Damascus for a holiday," she often said; "Come and see my poor gnarled roots." The summer of 1988 was the first time I could say yes.

During one of our earlier day trips we went by car along the valley of the Barada River, along the road I remembered from my first visit to the city. On our return, we left the ochre, tree-lined valley and took a new

road which sliced through the limestone of Jebel Qassyoun, the mountain which rises up behind Damascus.
The road was a short-cut back to the city. My thighs
and back were heat-stuck to the car seat and I felt my
face furrow against the light. Magnified by rock dust
and exhaust, the afternoon sun hung like Lucifer fallen
from heaven. As we crossed the shoulder of the mountain, we could see the presidential palace. Foursquare,
mighty, forbidding, the building dominated the city.
Then, as we passed the massive entrance gate, I corrected myself: it wasn't known as the presidential
palace, but The People's Palace—*Qasr el Sha'ab*. A couple of days earlier Hazar had made her thoughts clear
about this euphemism.

It was she too who had pointed to the small groups
of men cutting blocks of marble to build high front walls
along the pavements, screening the buildings behind.
"They decided Damascus needed a facelift and the next
thing you know it's happening." The men were covered
from head to toe in white dust, with *keffiyyah* scarves
wrapped round their faces to keep the worst of the grit
from their lungs. In the poorer quarters where the
houseowners couldn't afford the stone or the stonecut-
ters' wages, mud walls had been whitewashed, "to show
willing," Hazar said and smiled bitterly. By contrast, she
didn't mention the young men in open-necked shirts and
tight jeans who stood at every major intersection, each
one cradling a machine gun in his arms. But one morning she'd turned to me as we'd waited for traffic lights to
change on Abu Rumaniyeh and said, "You know, everyone who walks down a street in this city is complicitious
with the regime."

At just that moment a white Mercedes, throbbing
with sound, pulled up next to us at the lights. The driver
was a peacock of a man. He gave us the once over, lost interest and watched his friend, another slick-looking guy,
mime a lewd dance to the blaring music. When the lights
changed, their tires shrieked and we could see the young
men laugh as their car roared off down the street.

Hazar put her hand on my arm. "If you ever get frightened here, scream your lungs out and you'll be safe." She paused, then grinned at my puzzlement. "Only the very well-connected call attention to themselves." I looked at Hazar, then realized this was the other side of something she'd said earlier: that the streets of Damascus are as safe as houses because no one dares to commit a crime.

Another day we made our way to the *souq el Hamadiyyah* where for millennia the merchants of Damascus have traded luxuries, foodstuffs, arms. We'd gone in search of the scratchy bath cloths I remembered fondly from Turkey—bath cloths used in the *hammam* to peel off dead brown layers of skin. After searching the labyrinth of stalls and alleyways, we came to the Roman colonnade at the end of the covered market and walked out into the blindingly whitewashed square surrounding the Great Omayyid Mosque.

"Oh God," Hazar had winced, stopped in her tracks, and stared. "I haven't been here for ages. But I've heard about this. Look at those kitschy gaslights," she said, "they belong in a shopping mall in the States." Then she added, "It's the Ministry of Tourism and a bunch of tidy-minded do-gooders who are doing this."

It was in the mosque that Hazar started on the business with the heads: John the Baptist's head in a casket near the door and, farther inside, a whole shrine for the head of Huseyn. Then she remembered there was another head in the Great Mosque in Aleppo which belonged to the father of John the Baptist. "Poor Zacharius," she laughed, "his head was stuck behind green Perspex and a metal grill. First public degradation, then execution," she declaimed, "then guess what?" her voice rasped in my ear, "abracadabra, and a severed head becomes a holy relic!"

"Have you noticed the portraits of the President which grace our city?"

I remember nodding faintly. The portraits of the President lined the streets and filled every shop window.

Hazar had already made a point of driving past the enormous portrait which looked out on the city from the back of a Ministry building.

"So what are we to make of the fact that the holy heads come in singles, but Asad's head comes in multiples and repeat prints: twenty identical Asads wearing sunglasses and an army beret strung across Malky Boulevard at ten-meter intervals; six large Asads in his politician's suit across the front of the Meridian Hotel. A collage of video Asads, benign, nodding every night before the News on Syrian TV. And, the biggest Asad of all ready to take off and fly above Damascus from the back of the Ministry of Aviation."

By this time we were walking across the magnficent interior courtyard of the Great Mosque. A small flock of white doves flew up from the glittering Treasury building to the top of the minaret known as the Bride's Tower, but Hazar didn't notice them. She'd become more preoccupied and intense as she talked.

"It is as if the President's portraits are sacred. I'm sure they are there to remind us of the *mukhabarat*," she said. I thought of the unseen eyes of the secret police and realized that she'd not raised her voice above a barely audible whisper.

"He's a hydra. Big Brother. But why does his gaze never meet your eye?" And suddenly, from the fearsome edge to Hazar's voice, I understood that all she wanted from me was to let her vent her anger. It was an anger generated by being in Damascus, a rage I met later in other friends.

Sometimes it wasn't anger, but something else which would burst out of Hazar. It happened when she got us lost taking me to see the camps, the *mukhayyam*, where Palestinian refugees had settled in waves since 1948. Because there were no good maps of the city, I was useless as we drove round, dodging kids playing football, trying to find the main road again. On one of our circles, we passed a huge sign over a small corner shop.

"It says *jerabaat el qaraaseen*," Hazar laughed, then laughed so hard she had to slow the car and pull over to the side of the road. "Do you know what that means?"

I shook my head.

"It means 'The Pirates' Socks.'" Still shaking with laughter, she got out of the car and walked back to have a look inside. "They really do sell socks," she said when she returned, and crumpled into the car in a giggling heap.

"What does *jerabaat el qaraaseen* mean to you?" she asked her cousin Said when eventually we found our way home.

"Socks smuggled in from Lebanon?" Then he turned to Hazar in a moment of pure delight, "Do you remember seeing Burt Lancaster in *The Crimson Pirate?*" She nodded, shiny-eyed, then asked me if I'd seen it too.

As far as I could see, there was never any more sense to make of the pirates' socks than that, but its absurdity became a standing joke between us. The pirates' socks became one of those quirky moments which make a friendship and fundamentally alter the way we see the world. Such moments are precious anytime; they are moments when interest and sympathy become empathic. Such moments are often of great importance in the conduct of fieldwork and in the later theoretical and emotional dispositions the anthropological writer assumes, yet they are moments which, perhaps because they have the feel of fiction, rarely find a place in an ethnographic monograph.

In Spectacular Fashion: Fieldwork among *el tabaqeh el malekeh*, the Owning-Class

Hazar's friendship brilliantly colored my first weeks in Damascus. During this time, I also made other friends who were to play important roles in my fieldwork. Among them was Belqis, a woman whose address a mutual friend had given me in London. When I first met

Belqis I carefully explained how I wanted to study changing ideas of gender and marriage, but this time, instead of telling me a parable about delicacy and political intent, Belqis listened, then grinned, jumped up and grabbed my hand.

"If you really want to study Damascene marriage customs, then you must see a wedding reception at the Sheraton. I'll introduce you to the General Manager." And she did, that very evening. As his guest, I stayed on at the hotel to watch my first Sheraton poolside wedding. After that, my worthy plan to work among ordinary working folk of the city fell by the wayside: the chance to study such lavish weddings in anthropological terms was too intriguing to resist.

I knew that in the Arab world marriage ceremonies generally play a central part in people's lives: in the expense involved, the amount of time devoted to the ceremonies, the numbers of people who attend, the deep emotions aroused, and the complexity of the marriage customs. I also knew from my previous work that a study of changing marriage ceremonies would be an excellent point of entry for exploring wider changes in the political and economic environment. A single evening at the Sheraton was enough to confirm that in Syria, as in many other parts of the world, marriage ceremonies have become both more elaborate and increasingly similar in their outward features: it is a phenonmenon which raises fascinating questions about global economic and political processes, consumerism, and the movement of people, ideas, and things.[3]

Later I was introduced to the managers of the other five-star hotels in Damascus and, at the beginning of my study, I worked through these managements. Slowly I also built up a circle of families and friends whom I visited at home. Although many of these people were well-to-do, none of them were among the richest or most powerful in the country. They did, however, sometimes go to wedding receptions also attended by members of the ruling clique. By the end of my fieldwork I sometimes attended wedding receptions as a guest of the hotel, sometimes as a guest of the sponsors. I went to some weddings with groups of friends, while others I attended alone as a rather peculiar kind of journalist.

Studying Up

Initially, I had grave doubts about the whole project. I dislike in myself and others the very elitist attitudes I wanted to study. And, although in part I share the claims to taste, manners, and good education by which some of the well-to-do distinguished themselves and disparaged the new rich, there were few ways of accommodating my leftist/green politics from home. Moreover, I am a puritanical consumer and this, coupled with my relative poverty, made it difficult for me to subcribe easily to the predictable material comforts the people I met sought, valued, and could easily afford.

Differences in personal circumstances seemed to exaggerate the divide between myself and my Syrian friends. I had a full-time academic job for the sake of which I had chosen to leave my family for several months at a time to pursue research. Meanwhile in Damascus no family's reputation was impugned by my activities and I found myself with an extraordinary degree of personal autonomy. For some women and men my freewheeling position was enviable and a model which other women, or people generally, might emulate. Others saw me as threatening. Some women saw me as a rival, for others I clearly represented an unwelcome challenge to accommodations they had unwillingly made. Some men treated my presence as a chance to reveal daringly their subscription to "Western" values of social and sexual openness; others regarded me as a subversive who might encourge "their" women to change and used my presence as an excuse for diatribes against women's liberation.

In effect my political socialization in the field began with the fragmentation of my own perception of my identity as a female academic, while the people I came to know best fell into three rather different, but overlapping, groups.

My Women Friends: *Haute Bourgeois* and Middle-Aged

As an academic I gained entry into the company of several different groups of well-educated, but domesticated middle-aged women. At first, these women were very much "Others" in terms of how I saw myself as a university teacher and as a wife-and-mother. I found what I initially thought of as their bourgeois complacency unattractive and too familiar: they seemed very conservative and too much like the kind of woman whom I would have studiously avoided in Britain.

However, when they talked of what Kandiyoti (1988) would call their "patriarchal bargains"—the choices and compromises they made for the sake of their own and their children's domestic security and comfort—we found common ground. Some of the bargains they had made, bargains which defined the parameters of their everyday lives and their relations to others as wives, mothers, kinswomen, neighbors and friends, were very like those I'd also made.

But what was familiar in outline had Syrian specificities I had to learn to understand. In some cases, when I did, I easily shared the indignation of my friends: for example, their wry amusement and not infrequent distress at the gendered inequalities of the personal status laws, part of an Islamic legacy unchallenged by the socialist state. And there was much gossip about how women and men gained personal advantage by exploiting their sexuality or compromising business ethics. The titillation of salacious stories was coupled with censorious judgments. One aim of my fieldwork became to understand the compromises people made, how these were judged by others, and the wider authoritarian and patriarchal structures in which they were embedded.

The well-being of our children was another common bond, but here too the differences between us were also significant. I often found myself impatient with my friends' judgments of the success or failure of other people's children as an index of social worth. And I found it hard to accept the extent to which my friends allowed marriage choices to define social identity and privilege. Yet when discussions focused on the character and quality of the education available in Damascus, I shared my friends' anger at their limited choices: between the impoverished and militaristic schools in the state system and fiercely expensive private education in schools run by foreigners.

I followed my women friends as they involved themselves in a variety of charitable activities, civic associations, and flower-arranging groups. Most of them held regular visiting days and some were active members of French- and English-language reading circles. In one of these, Margaret Atwood's *Cat's Eye* (1990) was chosen for discussion. I was the same age as the other women of the reading circle and we found Atwood's descriptions of childhood fearfully and delightfully familiar.

What was more puzzling to me was the considerable discrepancy between spatial and spiritual mobility of Atwood's adult persona (which I felt I shared) and the lack of alternatives my friends felt they had or wanted. Some restrictions were self-imposed. Others were not, but were the consequences of state regulations on travel, the movement of currencies, and the difficulties other states made for Syrian nationals. More important but less tangible was how the interest and expectations of many of my middle-aged women friends became focused on a few highly controlled arenas, such as the wedding receptions. Here I did not sympathize easily with either the frenzied activity or the material competitions of the weddings, nor the need to keep up appearances at all costs, yet I knew I needed to understand how my friends evaluated success and acceptable degrees of political accommodation if my fieldwork was going to make any sense at all.

My "Seminar on Marriage"

My commitment to understanding the politics of marriage deepened through my relations with the second group I came to know well. Some of this second group of friends were the daughters and sons of the women of the first group. They were, to a degree, self-marginalized young women and men who felt themselves trapped between what they saw as Western ideals—such as companionate marriage—and the more calculated and controlling expectations of their families.

Throughout the fieldwork I was the catalyst for an ad-hoc gathering which was jokingly called my "seminar on marriage." Certainly my relation to the group had something of the character of teacher to students, but we all knew the real function of the marriage seminar was to provide an excuse for seeing friends and discussing topics, such as male bias and sexualities, unlikely to get an airing in other mixed gatherings. More importantly, the seminar gave us all a chance to learn how other people felt about dating, what they meant by successful marriage, and how they explained why relationships failed.

I understood some of the contradictions these friends saw themselves facing, something of the costs of their intransigence, and of the compromises they were expected to make. None of them felt willing or able to leave their families or Damascus. To me, their coping strategies seemed sometimes hilarious, sometimes maddening, and sometimes admirable. I commiserated, aided, and abetted whenever I could. And I have been honored by one remarkable woman who has credited me with some of the encouragement she needed to found and run her own school.

Certainly I became actively involved in the lives of friends from the seminar and I changed greatly in response to the personal dilemmas they described. My anthropological project, as conceived in terms of these friends, was to provide an account which focused on their personal aspirations and predicaments. Their politics were rarely radical, but centered on contested interpretations of domestic and familial authority. My input to these debates often involved raising wider questions about the character of the traps in which they felt themselves caught. As with the older women, my greatest interest was the differences between our various accounts of the relation between the personal and the political.

My Intellectual Friends

The third group with whom I spent a lot of time is perhaps easier to characterize. They were members of the dissaffected intelligensia who were highly critical of the state. For a variety of reasons, however, they declined to leave Syria for exile abroad. Some but by no means all of these people were scions of owning-class families who had chosen—often in the face of family pressure—to work in the arts, or as writers and translaters of demanding texts such as those of Foucault. With them I felt I shared many of my most cherished beliefs and interests. Certainly I felt with them that my whole personal and academic identity was on the line. My most useful function as a friend was as a procurer of books and critical reader of English language texts. With this group I was educated and actively politicized through their sophisticated critiques of the wider political economy. They encouraged me to use the main difference between us—nationality— and to address issues and audiences in ways they felt they could not (cf. Munif 1992; Kloos 1995).

The political perspectives I gained from my three groups of friends were quite different and often antithetical to each other (cf. Schrijvers 1991). However for me they all had a (somewhat illusory) common denominator. Roughly, the most villanous "others" that I learned to define during fieldwork were people whom my friends saw as acquiescent to the regime and its economic underpinnings. My friends' interest, and my own, was to explore what we meant by complicity and the degrees of compromise which they/I found avoidable and ultimately unacceptable. Provisional judgments about difference were contested and fluid. They were also the stuff of gossip—and jokes.

And there were lots of jokes. Jokes may be a measure of helplessness and a defense against despair, but they can also stand in for political discussion where free speech is denied. There were jokes about global politics: one from the summer of 1993 is still tragic and topical as this book goes to press—"Last week President Clinton was very angry and told the Serbs that if they didn't behave, he'd bomb Saddam Hussain." There were others about sexism and sectarian identities—"St. Peter and Jesus were enjoying a chat, when a man who'd just entered the Pearly Gates came up and asked, 'But where's Mary?' and Jesus looked around and shrugged then called out, 'Hey, Mama. Make the man a cup of Arab coffee.'" And there were others, crude jokes about the people from the city of Homs near the mountains north of Damascus. These were as sick as the Polack jokes in the States or the Bog Irish ones in England. I reckoned that these Homsi jokes were as close as many Syrians came to poking fun at the Alawites, President Asad's crowd.

My friends saw no unambiguous Others. The Sometimes Others included many of the very rich who were also closely associated with members of the inner circle of the regime, as well as Syrians and other Arabs who were members of transnational corporations. These Sometimes Others also included western ex-patriates working or doing research (like me), while yet others were employees in western governments, businesses, or universities (like me), whom my friends and I sometimes saw as both the missionaries and beneficiaries of neo-imperialism. Perceptions of Otherness were complex, confusing, and constantly shifting. The people with whom I did fieldwork were as aware as I was that we were all linked through networks of relations which defined a whole range of inequalities. With one friend in Damascus, I read chapters of Sharabi's treatise on neo-imperi-

144   *Dancing in Damascus*

alism, *Neopatriarchy: A Theory of Distorted Change in Arab Society* (1988). My friend Hazar was not alone in thinking that anyone, Syrian or not, who walked down the street was complicitous with the regime. Certainly my Otherness was sometimes directly implicated and challenged, but my friends too were sometimes seen as compromised and decried—by themselves, or their kin or friends—as Others who had sold out to the system. And, it was also the case that the motives and goals of the Sometimes Others were very familiar and all of us shared them, explicitly or covertly, on occasion.

Gender, Marriage, and the State: The Case of the Damascene Owning-Class

Constructions of identity and the ways they are related to degrees of loyality or anger and disagreement with the regime provide a focus for much of what I now want to say. In my fieldwork I sought to understand processes of gendering and notions of agency and choice in terms of the wider political economy, and to ask how individuals experience difference and inequality.

Dancing in Damascus ends with the story of Ghalia's Wedding, which is where my fieldwork began—at the grand wedding receptions in the five-star hotels, clubs, and private houses of Damascus. These celebrations are spectacular and extravagant. They are key rituals through which membership in the new owning class is defined. As one friend said to me, in English, and with a wicked grin: "They are the way we make status here in Damascus." Such new identities depend on wealth which derives, directly or indirectly, from connections with the ruling clique surrounding the Syrian president. But, because access to political and economic resources is unpredictable and always hidden in personal relations, individuals must make efforts to establish their own, and their family's importance, in other available currencies: "good" marriages and conspicuous consumption (cf. Tapper 1989/1990).

A central theme of the stories of *Dancing in Damascus* concerns the import of what Sharabi (himself an expatriate Syrian) has called "neopatriarchal" values (1988).[4] Sharabi argues that social privilege in the postindependence third world states depends on the skill with which people transform global styles into convincing local forms. For Sharabi, "neopatriarchy" represents a complex interaction between colonial/imperialist projects, such as the introduction of European educational and legal systems, and older Ottoman and Islamic ideologies and practices.

Typical of such neopatriarchal systems are a marked gender dichotomy and extreme emphases on heterosexuality and control of women. Another feature of such systems is what might be called the myth of the contemporary family. The discourse "on the family" (and its extension in ideas and practices of patronage) is complex. It fits well with extended, transnational business networks and the practices of marriage migration. Equally, the related notions concerning female virginity and chastity (see Lindisfarne 1994) have become an important means by which nationalism and Islamic identity are asserted, both internally and in the international arena.

In Syria, President Asad is often characterized as the father of his family, of the citizenry. Moreover, the family is bolstered as the unit of both social development and social control. The other side of this coin is that the family is seen as sacred—as the last preserve of privacy against state intrusion into personal and domestic lives. From an international perspective, other considerations are at work: from the way in which dependent states are often "feminized"[5] to the use of gendered violence to provide an incentive for military action (see Makiya 1993; cf. Hegland 1991).

Ethnographies of Middle Eastern elites are few. Most accounts are narrative political histories which tend to view elite formation in terms of a series of public events in which class and sectarian differences are treated as given. They ignore the activities of women, the relation between domestic and public lives, and the importance of cultural styles.[6] Yet, the processes by which elite identities are created and sustained are complex.

For example, it is in the interests of both men and women of the owning class to promote conspicuous consumption which unites consumerism and the rituals and experience of marriage. For many men, a system which treats women and some other men as elegant commodities provides them a public index of relative wealth and influence. This system also reinforces ideals of patriarchal authority in the household and elsewhere. Yet, within the owning class, these very structures of male dominance support the privileges of certain women.

The relationship between consumption and inequality is particularly important. The vastly expensive but least tangible acquisitions, such as education and travel, are highly valued among members of the owning class, but the relationship also finds material expression in other areas, such as house furnishing and women's charitable activities. And it is embodied in personal adornment and self-beautification. An aesthetics of "good taste" links the political economy of fashionable worth with the clothed body as a commodity and fashion as a performance art.[7]

The system, of course, has both its casualties and its rebels who refuse to bargain with patriarchy. People are aware of how the notions of love (variously romantic, familial, patriotic, and religious) mystify the relation between personal autonomy and authoritarian control. In particular, the lives of women without men are often tragic. Their stories reveal the mechanisms which ensure conformity to dominant ideals.

Neopatriarchal forms also trap people in marital disputes and domestic oppression. For example, while legal codes relating to political and economic affairs have been altered along western lines, it is notable that Syrian family law continues to be based closely on the Islamic Sharia, to the great disadvantage of women. It is also the case that the importance of patronage and the random exercise of force by the state have eroded the legal system. If the notion of "legal rights" is rendered meaning-less, there is little incentive to seek legal protection or to work for legal change. It is pertinent that a once lively feminist debate in Syria has been increasingly muted during the three decades of Asad's rule.[8]

The value of a study of social privilege depends on how power is understood. In this respect, Foucault's strictly relational approach to power is compelling. It un-settles an automatic association between power and the socially preeminent and focuses attention on social processes and historical specificities. However, as Norris (1992) points out, Foucault's account leaves no space for nuanced differences in ethical or political judgments. There is a strong argument which suggests that power is most clearly revealed through the experience of subordi-nation (see Scott 1990).

Behind my research, and the stories, lies such a perspective. One central theme I seek to explore is how discourses of "hegemonic masculinity" (Cornwall & Lin-disfarne 1994b, 1995)—that is, dominant idioms of mas-culinized power—benefit some men and women by systematically diminishing others. Idioms of masculin-ized power define inequalities (and gendered violence) between the first world and postcolonial states; between the ruling clique and others; between owning-class men and women and other Syrians; and within families be-tween those who are older and married and those who are junior and single.

Though the gendered idioms of domination are instru-ments of oppression, they can also be a source of hope. That is, dominant discourses on power may suppress, but never totally censor, people's awareness of everyday experi-ences of inequality. And because they are ideals which can never be wholly realized, they suggest their own opposites, offering scope for argument and dissent.

One of my aims in the field study was to describe the alternative, subordinate, and often muted voices within the owning class which challenged hegemonic formations and established authority. The stories are a product of this same ambition. As fiction, they afforded me a way of describing the historical specificity of the Syrian case, while retailing other features which suggest the wider connections between between global forms, nationalisms, and sexualities. And in my next book on Damascus, I hope to write of these things in a nonfiction style, for Syrian readers.

Abu Riyad's Second Story

In one sense, an academic description such as the one I've just offered can say it all. Or rather it says what can easily be said to academic readers in an academic style. What it omits, however, is the very stuff of the stories: a feeling for the people from whom the primary academic data were collected. It also preempts any wish, on the part of most Damascenes, to comment. Most of what is written in an ethnography is, for the ethnographic subjects, old hat. It is teaching your grandmother to suck eggs; or, as they say in Damascus, trying to sell water in the quarter of the water carriers. This was a lesson I learned early on, when my friend Hazar's father, Abu Riyad, told me a second story, this time about his war.

I was sitting on the balcony when Abu Riyad, looking cool and elegant in his long *jellabiyyah*, appeared carrying a tall frosty glass of *tut shami*. He must have known no one would ever refuse homemade mulberry sorbet. Then without a word of small talk, he sat down and began.

"I hated the dictators, Hitler, Mussolini, and the French, so when I was fifteen I ran off to fight with the British. But I didn't like the way they kept officers and men separate either. I went to Palestine and joined up there. The British took me and I spent five years in Egypt, Ethiopia, Tobruk, and then Salerno. Then I was told that if I went to India for six months, I'd be eligible for citizenship.

"Right through the war I served with a Scots major, a good man. But at the end, in Italy, an officer who'd just joined the regiment swore at me during a parade for being badly shaven. It was a pretext, an excuse to call me a "fucking Arab bastard." When he said that, I hit him—hard—and then went straight to our commanding officer and explained what I'd done.

"I was sent to the guardhouse. For a month my major kept urging me to speak to the lawyer. I refused; at the court martial, I would speak for myself.

"My defense was simple. I asked the general to read the first page of the Army regulations, the oath to King, flag, and uniform. Then I asked him what I was wearing. 'A uniform,' he answered. 'Yes,' I said, 'a uniform. And I hit the officer because he swore at this uniform.'

"Twenty minutes later, I was free and the officer was not." Abu Riyad got up and walked into the sitting room and I saw him carefully take a wad of tightly folded papers from a drawer in the bookcase.

"Look." He held them out to me. Among them were his discharge papers: he'd left the army honorably. I read out from the next bit of paper that the British army still owed him 325 Syrian pounds. Abu Riyad laughed.

"Later," he added, "I heard that the King's Regulations were changed, and if an officer swore at a soldier, it had to be followed up with a formal complaint, not fighting."

When he'd finished, there were flecks of story-gold shining in his eyes. Abu Riyad was challenging me to avoid presumption and patronizing ethnography. I knew then "writing-up" Damascus was going to be very tricky.

Fiction and Responsibility

My dilemma is of course familiar. Academics tend to write books with other academics in mind. While preaching to the converted may guarantee professional recognition and security, it is also likely to be a circular process, tedious to the insider and dismissed by others for its utter irrelevance to their lives. Writing fiction is one way of escaping this circularity. Fiction only works if the reader is engaged and entertained, while the aesthetics of the genre dictate that it is the reader who defines the import of a piece and the value of its insights on the world. Nonacademic audiences expect truths, the emotional and political truths which belong to fiction.

To write fiction is to insist on the subjective and constructed nature of all descriptive writing. It also requires the writer to relinquish all pretense to academic as opposed to writerly expertise. Further, with fiction comes an assertion that the writer, however she or he might be identified in other circumstances, has a legitimate right to describe the social lives of people anywhere, anytime. The paradox of course is that this very assertion of fictional autonomy seems to run headlong into orientalism. But perhaps this need not be so. Two issues are important here: the author's point of view and political intent.

A Syrian Identity?

The novelist Kheiri Dahabi in a recent public lecture in Damascus[9] discussed the ways in which Salman Rushdie could be said to "belong" to Britain, India and Pakistan, and, by analogy, which writers, whatever their background, might be said to be Syrian or Arab. Dahabi's argument was anti-essentialist and against any kind of identity politics. Dahabi argued that anyone writing in the language of particular people could be considered of that people, while any writer who, through whatever language, made a contribution to the cultural debates current in a particular setting might also be considered of that setting.

Identity politics depends on simple, reified representations based on color, sex, nationality, class, or cultural background. Such identities, either self-ascribed or imposed, become political "credentials" which can be used to legitimate the right to "speak for" those with whom one asserts a common identity and to silence others by a "more authentic-than-thou" attitude. Identity politics means that as a woman, or a member of a specific ethnic group, I can speak for all women or all members of my ethnic group, while "you"—with whom I share no common gendered or ethnic identity—have no right to speak. Such credentialism is often an essential part of rhetorics of difference which ascribe and naturalize the oppression of others.

Dahabi's strong argument against the assertion or ascription of fixed and immutable identities can be heard elsewhere. For instance, Eva Mackey's excellent paper "Revisioning 'Home'-Work" (1991), builds on what has been called a "revised politics of location," which is a feminist reaction to the frightening essentialisms of identity politics. Mackey synthesizes the points of view of a number of feminists when she suggests that all writing starts from "home," where "home" is simply "the place from where one begins" (1991: 9). She writes,

> All of these writers situate themselves firmly on shifting ground. They see the positions they speak from and write from as located in, and contingent upon, the very specfic context, always with the possibility for a different voice, a different reception. (1991: 7)

Put in terms of the ethnograpic writing debate, from whose point of view does the anthropologist report on fieldwork? For me there is now only one possible answer: I can only write from my own point of view. And my point of view has a history. It draws on the political dispositions I brought from "home." It is also a synthesis of the different ways my views from "home" were challenged, altered, and augmented in the field. My point of view also includes the extent to which I am now able and willing to find effective ways to share what I've learned.

In a sense I am simply arguing that the anthropologist, as both political actor and subject, is at the center of this descriptive and explanatory process. Inevitably, any account must be partial and subjective, but is also always political in a more formal sense. Its value, at least in part, must lie in the transparency of these conditions.[10]

Dissent and Surprise

For Dahabi, it is not a fixed identity which is important, but the character and quality of cultural intervention. His argument is not unlike that of Barbara Johnson, who has suggested grounds for literary criticism which sit well with what I would call "good practice" in anthropology. Johnson argues that the reading of a text is strong

> to the extent that it encounters and propagates the surprise of otherness. . . . How, then can one set oneself up to be surprised by otherness? Obviously, in a sense, one cannot. Yet one can begin by transgressing one's own usual practices, by indulging in some judicious time-wasting with what one does not know how to use, or what has fallen into disrepute. What the surprise encounter with otherness should do is lay bare some hint of an ignorance one never knew one had. . . . The surprise of otherness is that moment when a new form of ignorance is suddenly activated as an imperative. (1987: 15–16).

The trick of course, as Johnson knows, is to discover sustainable sources of curiousity and critical thought. One of these, for both the fictionist and the anthropologist, is an active commitment to dissent. This willful posture is necessary if one hopes to offer insights which go beyond the banal and the prejudices of the politically dominant. Such an attitude of dissent depends largely on two things:

affirming people's right to make choices for themselves, and a commitment to understanding how forms of resistance relate to an absence of choice. Such dissent also turns on several other premises. As Rabinow has put it,

> We change ourselves primarily through imaginative constructions. The kind of beings we want to become are open, permeable ones, suspicious of metanarratives; pluralizers. (1986: 257)

Christopher Davis, writing of changing identifications during fieldwork, writes of intervention, of how she offered an alternative interpretation to a friend's dream which, to her delight and surprise, was taken up and acted upon by the friend.

> From an ethnographic perspective, this is the type of event that verified the method; that founds or grounds our faith in it. The knowledge built up over months (and/or years); first of language, then of culture, then of particular histories; allows for the development of a capacity to adequately intervene in social life. By this, I mean an intervention which is good enough to be taken for what it says/does rather than to be remarked upon, laughed at, misunderstood, simply ignored or otherwise taken as an object and so removed from the exchanges in social life that make things happen between people.
> Biti [Davis's friend] received what was said, my foreignness receded and was no obstacle, my guise was real enough to live on. At that moment, the capacity of ethnography to bring one into the truth of things was verified for me; including verification of the unstable or ephemeral nature of that truth. The truth was in the chance insight and in the change, from one interpretation to another that it produced. (1993: 42)

Writing fiction is another form of personal and public intervention. It is a way of giving value to the insights of fieldwork, while accepting fully authorial responsibility. Fiction makes no claims, outside the constraints of the genre, to expertise or authority. It works when people read it with enthusiasm and willy-nilly find themselves engaged by the story.

The gambles in writing *Dancing in Damascus* have been of two kinds: whether or not I could unlearn the constraints of academic writing and whether or not my fieldwork was good enough to create believable Damascene characters and a Damascene world. My hope was that if I were successful, writing stories would unsettle any assertions of absolute difference between me and my readers and thus unsettle the racist categories which lurk behind national, ethnic, and sectarian difference.

I also had another ambition for my writing. It is conventional wisdom that via fiction a writer may say what would otherwise be censored. But the argument is, I think, more complex. What the Syrian writer Mamdouh Adwan has recently said about historical fiction[11] can also be said of ethnography:

> People argue that writers use history to avoid censorship, but no, this is not the case. We go to history to deepen the dialogue, an activity which is much more dangerous.

For Adwan, the notions of dissent and surprise are more than criteria for judging the value of fictional writing. He writes explicitly, he says, with the intention to scandalize: to make people think about their lives and their families, to shift boundaries, broaden horizons, and to alert them to the absences in their lives.

"Do you remember when we drove round and round in the *mukhayyam*, the Palestinian camps?" Hazar asked me toward the end of my first stretch of fieldwork in Damascus.

"Yes."

"Well, there are other refugees here too, but they're not allowed to call themselves that. They're from Quneitra and the Golan Heights. Officially they're known as 'the displaced,' *naaziheem*. They're people who can find no refuge at home."

Then she drew in a quick, deep breath. "Sometimes I feel like that too," and I thought, yes, and there but for the grace of God go all of us.

It was at that moment with Hazar when I first knew then that I wanted to write ethnography in a new way, that I wanted a power to surprise which academic writing necessarily lacks. And I liked the idea of writing short stories. As Toni Cade Bambara said of the form, "It makes a modest appeal for attention, allowing me to slip up alongside the reader and grab'm" (see Busby 1995).

NOTES

1. Research among the Shahsevan was carried out in the summers of 1965 and 1966 (see Tapper 1978, 1980). The greater portion of all my later research was supported by the Economic and Social Research Council (earlier the Social Science Research Council) of the United Kingdom whose generosity I gratefully acknowledge.

In 1970–72, my research in Afghanistan was funded as SSRC Project HR 1141/1, with Richard Tapper; see Tapper 1991), as was my study, "Women and Religion in a Turkish Town" (SSRC Project HR 7410; see Tapper 1985, 1990, 1990/1991; Tapper & Tapper 1987, 1988). The School of Oriental and African Studies supported my initial research visit to Syria in 1988 (see Tapper 1988/1989). In 1989–1990, I received a grant from the ESRC for research about "Changing Marriage Ceremonial and Gender Roles in Metropolitan Syria" (Project ROOO 23 1533) and its later writing up (ESRC Senior Research Fellowship, H524 27 5029 95). I also received support in 1996 for the writing project from the Nuffield Foundation.

Many people—family and friends, acquaintances and strangers—gave me much help and encouragement throughout my fieldwork and afterward. Some of them prefer not to be named, so it is better to mention no one. I thank them all from the bottom of my heart for the goodwill, energy, insights, and love they have shared with me.

2. Friends in Damascus, and Leila Zaki Chakravati in London, acquainted me with the novels of Ghada al-Samman, Hani al-Raheb, Collette al-Khoury and others whose writing became an important source for my work. In English translations, see the short story collections by Azrak (1988) and Badran and Cooke (1990), the stories of Zakariya Tamir (1985),

157

autobiographical and other novels by Hanna Mina (1993), Hanan al-Shaykh (1989, 1996), Salma al-Haffar Kuzbari (1992), Samar Attar (1994), Ulfat Idilbi (1995), Ghada Samman (1995), and Rafik Schami (1995), among others. See also Kaouk (1982) and McKee (1996) for critical discussions of Syrian and Levantine women writers and women in fiction. A wide range of Arab women's writing is now widely available in English translation.

3. On the similarities between weddings around the world, compare, for example, the work of Edwards (1989) with that of Charsley (1991) or Mai Zaki Yamani (1990, 1997).

4 Compare Suad Joseph's comments that studies of Middle Eastern women have paid little attention to the analysis of systems of production, class, colonial domination, capitalist penetration, urbanization, and state systems (1986: 502).

5. See, for example, Thaiss's discussion of this process with respect to Iran (1978).

6. Compare, for example, Philip Khoury's historical study of Syria and the French Mandate (1987) or Patrick Seale's more controversial biography of President Asad (1988) with the range of topics covered Abner Cohen's classic anthropological study of the elite in Sierra Leone (1981) or in Ghada Samman's shocking novel *Beruit '75* (1995). Elsewhere too writing on Middle East elites is uneven. Thus with respect to Saudi Arabian elite, compare the excellent investigative journalism of Aburish (1994), the anthropological studies of Soraya Altorki (1986) and Mai Yamani (1990, 1997) and the novels of Hanan el Shaykh (1989) and Hilary Mantel (1997) which describe the Saudi elite from expatriate points of view. Other useful models for anthropological studies of the *haute bourgeoisie* include McDonough's on Barcelona (1986) and Lomnitz and Perez-Lizaur's study of a Mexican family (1987).

7. Compare Bourdieu, 1984 *Distinction: A Social Critique of the Judgement of Taste* with Stauth and Zubaida's study of popular culture in the Middle East (1987). Appadurai's *The Social Life of Things* is an important starting part (1986), while Strathern (1988) and Grosz (1990) are particularly interesting on people, and body parts, as commodities.

8. See Shabaan (1988); cf. Kandiyoti (1991).

9. Kheiri Dahabi, "The Sources of the Fantastical in Arab Writing," a public lecture at The Arab Writers' Union, 8 April 1996, Damascus, Syria.

10. See Lindisfarne (1997a) and compare Marcus (1997) on the implicit political imperatives of multisited fieldwork, and Scheper-Hughes (1995) on the militant anthropology that is "good enough."

11. Mamdouh Adwan, "How Literature Deals with History," Third Cultural Season Lecture, The ESP Center, University of Damascus, 11 April 1996.

REFERENCES

Abu Lughod, Lila. *Writing Women's Worlds: Bedouin Stories.* Berkeley: University of California Press, 1993.

Aburish, Said K. *The Rise, Corruption and Coming Fall of the House of Saud.* New York: St. Martins, 1994.

Al-Haffar Kuzbari, Salma. *Lover after the Fiftieth.* Damascus: Tlas, 1992.

Al-Shaykh, Hanan. *Women of Sand and Myrrh.* London: Quartet, 1989.

―――. *Beirut Blues.* London: Vintage, 1996.

Altorki, Soraya. *Women in Saudi Arabia: Ideology and Behavior among the Elite.* New York: Columbia University. Press, 1986.

Appadurai, Arjun. *The Social Life of Things: Commodities in Cultural Perspective.* Cambridge: Cambridge University Press, 1986.

Asad, Talal (ed.), *Anthropology and the Colonial Encounter.* London: Ithica, 1973.

Attar, Samar. *Lina: A Portrait of a Damascene Girl.* Washington: Three Continents, 1994.

Atwood, Margaret. *Cat's Eye.* London: Virago, 1990.

Azrak, Michel (trans. and ed.). *Modern Syrian Short Stories.* Washington: Three Continents, 1988.

Badran, Margot, and Mariam Cooke (eds.). *Opening the Gates: A Century of Arab Feminist Writing.* London: Virago, 1990.

Bourdieu, Pierre. *Distinction: A Social Critique of the Judgement of Taste*. Cambridge, Mass.: Harvard University Press, 1984.

Busby, Margaret. "Toni Cade Bambara: In Celebration of the Struggle." *The Guardian*, (12 December 1995): 16.

Carrithers, Michael. "The Anthropologists as Author. Geertz's 'Works and Lives.'" *Anthropology Today* 4, no. 4 (1988): 19–20.

Charsley, Simon. *Rites of Marrying: The Wedding Industry in Scotland*. Manchester: Manchester University Press, 1991.

Chatila, Khalil. *Le Mariage chez les Musulmans en Syrie*. Paris: Paul Geuthner, 1934.

Clifford, James and George Marcus (eds.). *Writing Culture: The Poetics and Politics of Ethnography*. Berkeley: University of California Press, 1986.

Cohen, Abner. *The Politics of Elite Culture: Explorations in the Dramaturgy of Power in a Modern African Society*. Berkeley: University of California Press, 1981.

Cohn, Bernard. *An Anthropologists among the Historians and Other Essays*. Delhi: Oxford University Press, 1987.

Cornwall, Andrea, and Nancy Lindisfarne (eds.). *Dislocating Masculinity: Comparative Ethnographies*. London: Routledge, 1994a.

———. "Dislocating Masculinity: Gender, Power and Anthropology." In Andrea Cornwall and Nancy Lindisfarne (eds.), *Dislocating Masculinity: Comparative Ethnographies*. London: Routledge, 1994b, pp. 11–47.

———. "Feminist Anthropologies and Questions of Masculinity." In Akbar Ahmad and Cris Shore (eds.). *The Furture of Anthropology: Its Revelance to the Contemporary World*. London: Athlone, 1995: 134–157.

Daghestani, Kazem. *Etude Sociologique sur la Famille Musulmane Contemporaine en Syrie*. Paris: Ernest Leroux, n.d. (c. 1930).

Davis, Christopher. "Critical Fictions: Ethnography, Identity and the Open Work." Paper presented at the Anthropology Department Seminar, School of Oriental and African Studies, 1993: 1–45.

Edwards, Walter. *Modern Japan Through Its Weddings: Gender, Person, and Society in Ritual Portrayal.* Stanford: Stanford University Press, 1989.

Faludi, Susan. *Backlash. The Undeclared War Against American Women.* New York: Doubleday, 1991.

Gilsenan, Michael. *Lords of the Lebanese Marches: Violence and Narrative in an Arab Society.* London: I.B. Tauris, 1996.

Glass, Charles. *Tribes with Flags: A Dangerous Passage through the Chaos of the Middle East.* New York: Atlantic Monthly Press, 1990.

Grosz, Elizabeth. "Inscriptions and Body-maps: Representations and the Corporeal." In T. Threadgold and A. Cranny-Francis (eds.). *Feminine, Masculine and Representation.* London: Allen & Unwin, 1990.

Hegland, Mary. 1991. "Sexual Violence and Military Might: Mixed Metaphors of the Gulf War." Paper presented to the American Anthropological Association, Chicago, 1991: 1–36.

Idilbi, Ulfat. *Sabriya: Damascus Bitter Sweet.* London: Quartet, 1995.

Johnson, Barbara. *A World of Difference.* Baltimore: Johns Hopkins Press, 1987.

Joseph, Suad. "Study of Middle Eastern Women: Investment, Passions and Problems." *International Journal of Middle East Studies* 18, no. 4 (1986): 501–509.

Kandiyoti, Deniz. "Bargaining with Patriarchy." *Gender and Society* 2, no.3 (1988): 274–290.

———. (ed.). *Women, Islam and the State.* London: Macmillan, 1991.

Kaouk, Layla Ida. *La Femme dans le Roman Syrien, 1967–1977.* Paris: Unpublished These de Doctorat 3em cycle en Sociologie, Ecole des Hautes Etudes en Science Sociales, 1982.

Khoury, Philip. *Syrian and the French Mandate: The Politics of Arab Nationalism, 1920–1945.* Princeton: Princeton University Press, 1987.

Kloos, Peter. "Publish and Perish. Nationalism and Social Research in Sri Lanka." *Social Anthropology* 3, no. 2 (1995): 115–128.

Lieve, Joris. *The Gates of Damascus.* Melbourne: Lonely Planet, 1996.

Lindholm, Charles. "The New Middle Eastern Ethnography." *Journal of the Royal Anthropological Institute* 1, no. 4 (1995): 805–820.

Lindisfarne, Nancy. "Variant Masculinities, Variant Virginities: Rethinking 'Honour' and 'Shame'." In Andrea Cornwall and Nancy Lindisfarne (eds.). *Dislocating Masculinity: Comparative Ethnographies.* London: Routledge, 1994, pp. 82–96.

———. "Local Voices and Responsible Anthropology: Finding a Place from which to Speak." *Folk, Journal of the Danish Ethnographic Society* 39 (1997a): 5–25.

———. *Al Raqs fi Dimasq.* (Trans. Mamdouh Adwan) Damascus: Dar al Mada, 1997b.

———. "The Box (1959)." *Anthropology Today* 13, no. 5 (1997c): 13–18.

———. "The Tortoise." *Anthropology and Humanism 23,* no. 1 (1998): 83–90.

Lindisfarne-Tapper, Nancy. "Local Contexts and Political Voices," *Anthropology in Action* 10 (1991): 6–8.

Lomnitz, Larissa and Marisol Perez-Lizaur. *A Mexican Elite Family, 1820–1980.* Princeton: Princeton University Press, 1987.

Mackey, Eva. "Revisioning 'Home'-work: Feminism and the Politics of Voice and Representation." Unpublished paper, 1991: 1–18.

Makiya, Kanan. *Cruelty and Silence: War, Tyranny, Uprising and the Arab World.* London: Jonathan Cape, 1993.

Mantel, Hilary. *Eight Months on Ghazzah Street*. New York: Henry Holt, 1997.

Marcus, George. "Some Strategies for the Design of Contemporary Fieldwork Projects: Advice to New Students." *Ethnologia* (Lisbon) 6–8 (1997): 55–64.

McDonough, Gary. *Good Families of Barcelona*. Princeton: Princeton University Press, 1986.

McKee, Elizabeth. "The Political Agendas and Textual Strategies of Levantine Women Writers." In Mai Yamani (ed.). *Feminism and Islam*. New York: New York University Press, 1996: 105–140.

Mina, Hanna. *Fragments of Memory: A Story of a Syrian Family*. Austin: University of Texas Press, 1993.

Mohanty, Chandra Talpade. "Feminist Encounters: Locating the Politics of Experience." In Barrett, Michele and Anne Phillips (eds.). *Destabilizing Theory: Contemporary Feminist Debates*. Oxford: Polity Press, 1992, pp.74–92.

Moors, Annelies, "Women and the Orient: A Notes on Difference." In Nencel, Lorraine and Peter Pels (eds.). *Constructing Knowledge: Authority and Critique in Social Sciences*. London: Sage, 1991, pp. 114–122.

Munif, Abdur Rahman. "Moving Beyond Lines in Sand." *The Guardian* (14th April 1992): 21–22.

Nader, Laura. "Up the Anthropologist—Perspectives Gained from Studying Up." In D. Hymes (ed.), *Reinventing Anthropology*. New York: Pantheon, 1969, pp. 284–311.

Nicholson, Linda. *Feminism/Postmodernism*. London: Routledge, 1991.

Norris, Christopher. *Uncritical Theory: Postmodernism, Intellectuals and the Gulf War*. London: Lawrence & Wishart, 1992.

Pels, Peter. "Professions of Duplicity: Towards a Hisotry of Anthropological Ethics." Paper presented at the EASA Workshop, "Ethics and Politics of Anthropological Research: Changing Paradigms." Barcelona, (1996), 1–36.

Rabinow, Paul. "Representations are Social Facts: Modernity and Post-Modernity in Anthropology." In James Clifford and George Marcus (eds.). *Writing Culture: The Poetics and Politics of Ethnography.* Berkeley: University of California Press, 1986, pp. 234–261.

Rabo, Annika. *Change on the Euphrates.* Stockholm: Studies in Anthropology, 1986.

Said, Edward. *Orientalism.* London: Routledge & Kegan Paul, 1978.

————. "Representing the Colonized: Anthropology's Interlocutors." Critical Inquiry 15 (1989):205–225.

Samman, Ghada. *Beirut '75.* Fayetteville, University of Arkansas Press, 1995.

Schrijvers, Joke. "Dialectics of a Dialogical Ideal: Studying Down, Studying Sideways and Studying Up." In Lorraine Nelcel and Peter Pels (eds.). *Constructing Knowledge: Authority and Critque in Social Science.* London: Sage, 1991, pp. 162–179.

Scott, James. *Domination and the Arts of Resistance.* New Haven: Yale University Press, 1990.

Scheper-Hughes, Nancy. "The Primacy of the Ethnical: Propositions for a Militant Anthropology." *Current Anthropology* 36, no. 3 (June 1995): 409–420.

Seale, Patrick. *Asad.* London: I.B. Tauris, 1988.

Shabaan, Bouthaina. *Both Right and Left Handed: Arab Women Talk about Their Lives.* London: Women's Press, 1988.

Schami, Rafik. *Damascus Nights.* New York: Scribner, 1995.

Sharabi, Hisham. *Neopatriarchy: A Theory of Distorted Change in Arab Society.* Oxford: Oxford University Press, 1988.

Stauth, Georg and Sami Zubaida (eds.). *Mass Culture, Popular Culture, and Social Life in the Middle East.* Boulder, Colorado: Westview Press, 1987.

Strathern, Marilyn. *The Gender of the Gift.* Berkeley: University of California Press, 1988.

Tamer, Zakiriyya. *Tigers on the Tenth Day*. London: Quartet, 1985.

Tapper, Nancy. "The Women's Sub-Society among the Shahsevan Nomads of Iran." In Lois Beck and Nikki Keddie (eds.). *Women in the Muslim World*. Cambridge, Mass.: Harvard University Press, 1978, pp. 374–398.

———. "Matrons and Mistresses: Women and Boundaries in Two Middle Eastern Tribal Societies." *European Journal of Sociology* 21 (1980): 58–78.

———. "Changing Wedding Rituals in a Turkish Town." *Journal of Turkish Studies* 9 (1985):305–313.

———. "Changing Marriage Ceremonial and Gender Roles in the Arab World: An Anthropological Perspective." *Arab Affairs* 8 (Winter 1988/1999), 117–135.

———. "*Ziyaret*: Gender, Movement and Exchange in a Turkish Community." In Dale F. Eickelman and James Piscatori (eds.). *Muslim Travellers: Pilgreimage, Migration and Religious Imagination*. London: Routledge, 1996, pp. 236–255.

———. "'Traditional' and 'Modern' Wedding Rituals in a Turkish Town." *International Journal of Turkish Studies* 5, no. 1–2 (1990/1991): 135–154.

———. *Bartered Brides: Politics, Gender and Marriage in an Afghan Tribal Society*. Cambridge: Cambridge University Press, 1991.

Tapper, Nancy and Richard Tapper. "The Birth of the Prophet: Ritual and Gender in Turkish Islam." *Man* 21, no. 1 (1987):69–92.

Tapper, Richard and Nancy Tapper. "'Thank God We're Secular': Aspects of Fundamentalism in a Turkish Town." In Lionel Caplan (ed.). *Studies in Religous Fundamentalism*. London: Macmillan, 1988, pp. 51–78.

Taqalid al-zawaj fi'l-iqlim al-suri. Damascus: Ministry of Education, 1961.

Terjuman, Sirham. *Ya Mal al-sham*. Damascus: Ministry of Education, 1978.

Thaiss, Gustave. "The Conceptualization of Social Change Through Metaphor." *Journal of Asian and African Studies* 13, no. 1–2 (1978):1–13.

Wade, Peter (ed.). *Advocacy in Anthropology.* Manchester: The Group for Debates in Anthropological Theory, 1995.

Yamani, Mai Zaki. 1990. *Formality and Propriety in the Hejaz.* Unpublished D.Phil. Dissertation, Oxford University.

———. "Changing the Habits of a Lifetime: The Adaption of Hejazi Dress to the New Social Order." In Nancy Lindisfarne and Bruce Ingham (eds.). *Languages of Dress in the Middle East.* London: Curzon, 1997, pp. 55–66.